VINEET BAJPAI

MASTAAN

The Fallen Patriot of Delhi

TreeShade Books

www.treeshadebooks.com

Published by TreeShade Books (VB Performance LLP) in 2019

This is a work of fiction. Names, characters, places, institutions, organisations and events are either the product of the author's imagination or are used fictitiously. Any resemblance of any kind to any actual person living or dead is entirely coincidental.

The publisher and the author will not be responsible for any action taken by a reader based on the content of this book. This work does not aim to hurt the sentiments of any religion, class, sect, region, nationality or gender.

MASTAAN

The Fallen Patriot of Delhi

ISBN: 978-93-89237-04-7

Published by

TreeShade Books (VB Performance LLP)
Corporate Park, Sector 142, Noida
Uttar Pradesh - 201305, India
Email - publish@TreeShadeBooks.com
www.TreeShadeBooks.com

Printed and Bound in India by

HT Media Ltd. Gr. Noida

Cover Design by

Munisha Nanda

MASTAAN

The Fallen Patriot of Delhi

TreeShade Books

www.treeshadebooks.com

To my seven twinkling stars -
Vedika, Seher, Aditi, Samaya,
Vandita, Arshiya & Mira

Disclaimer

This is a novel, a work of pure imagination and fiction, written with the sole intention of entertaining the reader. While the content has several references to religion, history, institutions, historical characters, beliefs, myths and structures, it has been presented with the singular purpose of making the story richer and more intriguing. The author and the publisher are admirers of all faiths, religions and nationalities, and respect them equally and deeply. They make no claim to the correctness of the historical or mythological references and facts used in this novel. Names of some well-known historical characters have not been changed with the only objective of giving the tale a real-life flavor, and those characters have been given a strong fictional makeover for the purpose of story-telling only. The author and the publisher have no intention of offering any opinion on any individual either from the past or from the present. This book has been developed and produced by a vibrant multicultural team richly representing various faiths, beliefs, languages, regions, genders and ethnicities.

This book is dedicated to the
forgotten heroes of 1857 -
India's First War for Independence.

To the nameless, faceless thousands
who embraced martyrdom & scripted
the genesis of a Nation called India
with their blood.

Acknowledgements

As I wait nervously for the release of *Mastaan*, it is the most opportune time for me to express my heartfelt gratitude to the readers of the Harappa Trilogy, my first three fiction novels.

Whatever I am as an author today is because of the lacs of readers who not only loved *Harappa*, *Pralay* and *Kashi* boundlessly, but elevated the books to a cult status. Books of the Harappa Trilogy remain bestsellers till the date of the writing of this section, and every week I receive hundreds of emails, tweets and messages from my readers who shower me with their love. As further gratification, screen-rights of the books have been picked-up by none other than Reliance Entertainment, one of the most respected names in India's entertainment ecosystem. We hope to see the books on the big screen of cinema soon. My readers have embraced the books not only in the English language, but also in Hindi, Gujarati and Marathi. My indebtedness to them cannot be described in words.

Coming to *Mastaan*. My first big 'thank you' would be to the excellent team of my publisher, TreeShade Books. Thank you, Ruchika, Shobhit, Navin, Pawan, Devaraja, Vikram, Sharat and everyone else in the TreeShade team for your exceptionally professional and committed partnership. You supported me not just during the creative, editorial and print production of the book, but also in the pre-release marketing campaigns. You guys rock. Like totally.

A very special mention to the distribution partners of this title, Gaurav Sabharwal and team Prakash Books, for being an enormous strength and for being partners in progress. A big shout out to the teams of my advertising and digital-marketing agencies, Magnon eg+ and Magnon\TBWA, for offering world-class digital, advertising and social marketing solutions for the promotions of all my titles. You guys are, beyond doubt, the best in the business. Thank you, team Talentrack – your content-strategy and influencer-marketing campaigns have delivered exceptional results. Harini Srinivasan, my classy and fantastic Editor, please accept my gratitude for all the value you have added to this book. Thanks a million for making the manuscript better than what it was when it reached you.

My friend and superstar, Sid Jain from *The Story Ink* – a warm hug to you for taking my books to their true potential on the big glamorous screen of cinema. And for being the golden guy you are. The inimitable Namita Gokhale, thank you for your ever-brutal critiques but your ever-affectionate generosity. You are a treasure for India's scholarly canvas. Lipika Bhushan, Vivek Merani, Ayushi Srivastava, Iti Khurana, Munisha Nanda, Varun Bajpai... all of you are the sparkling planets of my literary solar system.

Coming to the glowing inspirations and the research sources that guided me during the writing of *Mastaan*. William Dalrymple, you are my all-time favorite and your magnificent books, *The Last Mughal* and *White Mughals,* were my principal research treasures. *Delhi: A Novel* by late Khushwant Singh was a priceless body of work that not only offered profound insights into the history of Delhi but also a romantic inventiveness to produce more literature around the great city. Thank you, Rana Safvi, for your enchanting book *City of My Heart*. It helped me understand the softer elements of the life and times of the splendid Mughal Capital of 1857. I cannot help but mention some timeless classics that gave me the overall research underpinning for *Mastaan* – the novel *Kim* by the great Rudyard Kipling; the unforgettable Doordarshan TV serial *Mirza Ghalib,* starring the brilliant Naseeruddin Shah and the immortal Jagjit Singh; and last but never the least, the ever-supreme *Amar Chitra Kathas*.

My literary initiatives would not have been a reality without the undying support of my colleagues and leaders from the iconic eg+ Worldwide, TBWA and Omnicom networks. Paul Hosea, Simon Toaldo, Alain Rhone, Paul Fothergill, Troy Ruhanen, Denis Streiff and Neeraj Puri – thanks a million for your affectionate encouragement. It means the world to me.

Finally, coming to my management team and my family – *I am what I am today because of all of you*. The names are too many to write here, but I think you know who you are. You give me the strength, the belief, the opportunity and the ambition to reach for the stars.

Utthishtha!

Rise!

Vineet Bajpai

Prologue

4th May, 1799 AD

'His body is still warm.

He… he is refusing to die… John *saahab*!'

As John McGowen struck the seemingly impregnable stoned floor yet again with his pickaxe, Muntasir Bakhsh shivered in the manner of a man possessed. His eyes were rolled up like those of an entranced *dervish* of yore, and his body trembled as if it were in the grip of a primordial *djinn* – clawing out from the dark depths of hell.

The nearly deranged young British officer of the East India Company did not flinch. Not anymore. He could die here tonight, in this ghostly dungeon, for all he cared.

My spirit will haunt this castle forever. If I don't acquire this cursed treasure tonight, no one ever will!

The Englishman had no idea how fateful this thought was going to turn out.

The cannons continued to roar in a devastating barrage, their iron slug-balls bouncing off the indestructible *praacheer* or fort-walls of Seringapatam, the stronghold of the Tiger of Mysore.

Such a coldblooded war had never been witnessed on earth before. Never had such a mammoth siege been laid around a castle.

'*Sher-e-Mysoor* is a living corpse... saahab,' Bakhsh persisted.

The profusely sweating John McGowen feigned nonchalance towards the words of his native accomplice and continued to feverishly slam the stubborn floor with his pickaxe. But deep down he was not immune to the horror those words carried. Not even remotely.

'It has been three hours since they stabbed him multiple times. You even shot him under his ear. And yet his body burns like embers... he... he... he is a ghost, John saahab...'

'Oh, just shut up, will you, Bakhsh? Shut up! Shut up! SHUT UP...!' screamed McGowen, pointing his finger ominously towards the bearded Mohammedan from the walled city of Delhi.

Convinced that he had silenced the foreteller of their inexplicable yet imminent doom, McGowen turned back to the arduous task of breaking further deep into the secret underground vault. What lay hidden below this last barrier was the known world's most priceless, unfathomable treasure.

The treasure of the Tiger.

The Tiger of Mysore.

The treasure of Tipu Sultan!

'He knows we are here... sneaking... stealing... defiling the treasure he so loved and nurtured all his life...' continued Muntasir Bakhsh in the hissing manner of an unscrupulous thief, now regretting the day he had agreed to embark upon the riskiest heist of all time. Only a mad man would dare to tread upon the Tiger's gold.

Just then the stoned floor gave way. Cracks appeared. John McGowen raised his excited, terrified eyes to look at his lone accomplice of this horrifying night. Despite the chilling fear Muntasir Bakhsh felt, at this moment even his face convoluted, overcome all over again by the insane lust that gold instils in the hearts and souls of men.

Instantly forgetting his terror and his laments, he grinned madly at John. Before long Muntasir joined him in bludgeoning through the last barrier between them and the world's most spectacular riches.

In less than thirty minutes, the two men smashed the final roadblock open and were clambering down the flight of stairs that lay revealed as the fruit of their courageous labor. The stairway seemed to lead into the darkest belly of the earth.

As they arrived at their ill-fated destination, what the two nearly lunatic men saw in the amber light of their flickering wicker-torches, was beyond their wildest imagination.

What they beheld in front of their dazzled eyes was the world's most immeasurable, unimaginable and blinding spectacle of wealth!

They laughed and laughed.

Hysterical with the breathtaking exhibition of diamonds, rubies, gold bars, coins, jewelry, statues made of solid gold, chests full of sapphire, gem-studded vases brimming with precious stones, ropes made of gold wire, gems of the size of pigeon-eggs, ancient artefacts, diamond studded swords... all spread over what looked like a hall with no boundaries, the Englishman from London and the *Hindustani* from Delhi went completely insane.

'You see... you see, you ol' blighter... *this* is what I have been telling you about! From this moment on, you and I will be the world's richest men!' yelled John in uncontrollable ecstasy.

What the young Brit had forgotten was that Tipu, the Emperor of Mysore, was still not gone. The Tiger's body had been disfigured by English swords and cartridges several hours ago. Any human corpse would have gone stone cold in a few minutes. But not Tipu. Even after four hours of the collapse of his mutilated body, Tipu's cadaver still scorched like a cauldron of hellfire.

He was watching them.

From his afterlife.

Tipu's tortured, enraged soul was now seeking a blood-sacrifice!

In the midst of what was a deathly silence, something stirred. It was like the rasping sound of rough stone grinding against a hard surface.

The two treasure-hunters exchanged petrified glances, before looking in the direction of the unnerving sound.

In their unhinged and premature celebration, John and Muntasir had missed a very important detail. The staircase that had led them to this treasure vault had ended in a stone-cut doorway. Almost ten feet in height and about four feet in its girth, this doorway was guarded by a sliding obelisk of a gate – precariously held up above a slippery channel. Stone floor-tiles of the cellar had been engineered to trigger the closure of this behemoth of a door when walked upon by unwelcome footsteps.

This massive door had begun to slide down, dropping several feet in one go. In an instant, the two men realized that a shutter of sorts, made of a single cut stone-block weighing several tonnes, was going to seal the vault for good. As dust blew from the groove and a more unnerving rumble announced the final drop of the stone colossus, the only two men to have ever entered the Tiger's treasure-vault uninvited, felt cold sweat all over their bodies.

This was Tipu's final trap for anyone who dared to enter his forbidden lair.

It was only now that they realized, to their cold horror, why Tipu was not leaving.

The Tiger of Mysore was lingering on for a purpose. Deep down in the dark, haunting cellars of his beloved Seringapatam Fort, alongside his fabulous wealth, the ghost of Tipu Sultan was going to entomb these two wretched men - *alive.*

For their *yaksha* or guardian-spirits to protect his cursed yet priceless treasure.

Forever.

Part 1

Kaun jaa.e 'Zauq'
par Dillī kī galiyāñ
chhoḌ kar

- SHEIKH IBRAHIM ZAUQ

Phaansi-gar

Delhi-Mathura Highway, December 1856

Their teeth chattered as they pressed on further into the dense forest, lush green with freshly washed foliage and enveloped by a foggy, icy mist.

The freezing cold of the outskirts of Delhi had worsened as an outcome of harsh, unseasonal rains in the month of December. Shivering under the onslaught of the extreme chill and the incessant downpour, *sipahi* or *sepoys* of the East India Company could barely keep a grip on their lances, rifles and muskets. The whiteness of their cold knuckles matched the anxious paleness of their tense faces, as they inched further into bandit country.

Straining his eyes against the sharp raindrops, as he led his company of Hindustani sepoys on foot, *Subedaar-Major* Chhagan Dubey tightened his grip on his service Brown Bess musket.

DHABBAAAAAAMM...!!

His powerful firearm roared, ripping through the eerie silence of the winter forest.

DHABBAAAAAAMM...!!

The very next moment he opened fire again into a distant thicket with his second musket, screaming a caution command so loud that his neck veins appeared ready to explode.

'PHAANSI-GAAAA...R!' he yelled, pointing in the direction of the undergrowth where he had spotted enemy movement.

Almost instantaneously, Lieutenant Robert D'Cruze, the Regiment Commander, pulled out his newly commissioned Colt revolver, and emptied all six of the gun's chambers in the direction that Chhagan had pointed towards. His trust on Subedaar-Major Chhagan was second only to his unquestioned faith on his force's most legendary warrior – who was currently leading a parallel pursuit, not far from where the D'Cruze Regiment was.

The sepoys also followed suit, opening fire a hundred rifles, and then charging with their bayonets and scimitars.

Hunt for the *Phaansi-gar* or the dreaded *Hangmen* had begun.

Phaansi-gar was another name for the notorious and cruel bands of dacoits and murderers who ravaged Northern India for hundreds of years – the *Thugs*!

Looting, robbing and killing unsuspecting traders, travelers and caravans since the 14th century, the Thugs were the most feared and despised bands of highway robbers and slaughterers. They had also wickedly earned the title of Phaansi-gar, because they were known to befriend travelers, drug them during meals and then 'hang' or strangle them to death using a *roomal* or a noose. A *phaansi*.

It was only as late as the 1830s that the then Governor General of the East India Company, Lord Willian Bentinck, decided to eradicate the malaise of *Thugee*. He deployed a massive army of soldiers and spies to outmaneuver the dacoits. But it was easier planned than executed. The Thugs were not just robbers murdering innocent travelers. They were large bands of organized and armed brigands, fully prepared to take on the might of the East India Company head-on.

It was an ambush.

Unaware that they were being lured into a bandit-stronghold deep inside the dense forest, Lieutenant D'Cruze, Subedaar-Major Chhagan Dubey and their soldiers charged into the depths of the jungle.

The Thugs were everywhere. Behind bushes, hidden in the thick of shrubbery, on tree-tops and perched atop hidden *machaans*. A hail of poison-tipped arrows, iron-grape crude bombs and country-made musket-shots greeted the sepoy company in what appeared to be an inescapable massacre. Twenty of the Hindustani soldiers fell in a matter of a minute or less.

Even though stunned momentarily at the brutal intensity of the Thug assault, the well-trained company of the D'Cruze Regiment soon regained its composure and scrambled for cover. The soldiers shot back at the bandits with the precision of the able marksmen that they were, inflicting some losses.

The ever-gallant Lieutenant D'Cruze had by now reloaded his revolver, even as his horse neighed in panic at the fiery chaos all around. He took the gun in his left hand and drew the sword strapped to his saddle with his right. He charged towards the enemy ranks fearlessly, shooting and slashing at the same time. Chhagan followed as well, closely on the heels of the young, decorated British officer.

But despite their renowned valor, today the D'Cruze Regiment was hopelessly outnumbered. The Thugs were in hundreds.

In the bloodbath and imminent death that surrounded them, every single sepoy of the company was now hoping for a miracle.

Their very own miracle.

The Wounded Timurid

Delhi, December 1856

The *Badshah* of Hindustan was old and angry.

He was a king with no kingdom. A ruler with no subjects. A monarch with no army.

And he was completely bankrupt.

The meeting appointment of the Badshah with the British Resident of Delhi was just an hour away.

More humiliation.

The *Khalifa* – theoretically God's appointed Regent and the supposed religious leader of all the Muslims of the entire planet, the Caliph - felt incapable of even getting out from his decaying bed of the once-opulent *khwaabgaah* (sleeping chambers) of the Great Mughals.

The octogenarian knew very well that the time for his mighty dynasty's demise had come.

But the shriveled *Timurid* – a direct descendant of the fearsome *Taimur Lang* or Timur the Lame - harbored a gnawing desire in his aging heart that only he knew of.

In vicious contrast to his soft and poetic exterior, the heart of the son of Akbar Shah the second still beat in the manner suited to the bloodline of Timur himself.

Bahadur Shah hated the British. Deep in the black recesses of his burning soul, he dreamed of beheading them and hanging their thrashing bodies publicly at the famous Gates of the walled city of Delhi.

'*Shukriya*, Tanzeem,' whispered the gentle old emperor to the *kaneez* (concubine) who served him his morning laxative prepared specially by Hakeem Ahsanullah Khan, the Badshah's trusted friend, physician and strategist.

There was no escaping the impending meeting. The British Resident of Delhi was a hard man – respectful in his words but scathingly insulting in his actions. Every meeting with him meant more and more concessions being snatched away from the Mughal grasp. Lower pension for the Badshah and his already poverty-stricken princes, fewer concubines, restricted palace access, lesser servants... and more unexpected penalties. The Resident doffed his hat and stood up from his seat in the presence of Bahadur Shah no doubt, but those acts of courtesy only added insult to injury.

Bahadur Shah appeared to be a frail, religious man. A poet. A gardener. A soft soul, incapable of even peaceful conflict, let alone war.

But underestimating the old king would be an enormous mistake.

I have never needlessly harmed even a fly in my life. But these firangis are the devil incarnate. The heathen ought to be punished for their deeds. If only I enjoyed the youth of my great ancestor Aurangzeb when he ascended the throne... if only I commanded the formidable armies of Taimur... every British soul in Dilli would burn in the fires of jahannum (hell).

Setting his far-fetched thoughts aside with a sigh, the tired king began to dress for the meeting.

Bahadur Shah was, above everything else, a wounded Timurid.

Never for a moment did he forget what his title truly meant.

He was *Zafar* - the Victorious.

He was Bahadur Shah Zafar!

'Leftinant Saahab...!'

Delhi-Mathura Highway, December 1856

Surrounded on all sides by the deafening explosion of crude bombs and the cracking of blazing muskets, drenched in sweat, blood and the freezing downpour, Lieutenant Robert D'Cruze was sorely regretting his decision.

Grossly undermining the strength of the Thugs, he had sent away his ablest warrior, his finest sepoy-commander to another territory, along with a legion of D'Cruze Regiment's most elite cavalry. The Lieutenant had sent away the one man who, over the years, had brought both fame and glory to the D'Cruze Regiment. The one man who could have changed the face of this increasingly hopeless battle... singlehandedly.

Fighting seven or eight Thugs simultaneously, the veteran Subedaar-Major Chhagan Dubey was convinced.

This is it.

He knew he was going to die this cold, rainy morning... at the hands of the cruel Phaansigar. The odds were insurmountable.

Each of the remaining sepoys was now surrounded by half a dozen bandits, the latter viciously attacking the men in red tunics with blades and knives, determined to kill every last one of the soldiers who had dared to enter their widely feared stronghold.

By now, even Chhagan was missing his best friend dearly – the man whom Robert D'Cruze had sent away. Fighting fiercely with a sword in one hand and a dagger in the other, the Subedaar-Major nurtured one last flicker of hope in his pounding heart.

He must have heard it by now. The guns... the crude bombs.

He must have heard it!

The Colt revolver fell from his hand as a bandit dagger tore through Robert D'Cruze's forearm. Despite the mayhem all around him, this young British officer was not one to retreat or to surrender easily. Nor was he a stranger to ambushes. He slashed furiously at the attacking Thug with his sword, instantly inflicting a mortal wound on the bandit.

But the sepoys were despairingly outnumbered.

Even as one brigand fell, around twenty Phaansigar appeared menacingly, and began to slowly encircle D'Cruze's horse. In no time, the officer of the East India Company was completely surrounded.

'Come on, you scoundrels... show me what you've got!' yelled the gritty Robert, as he prepared for what evidently seemed to be his last battle.

Just as he was deciding whether he should jump off from his mount and fight the Thugs on foot or not, something unexpected happened. In what appeared to be a storm of expertly fired rifle shots, almost all of the attackers were pushed back stumbling in different directions by a hail of streaking lead, each of them crashing on to the wet slush of the ground.

Lieutenant D'Cruze looked around in bewilderment, only to find his trusted Subedaar-Major staring at him from a distance, with wide, relieved and jubilant eyes.

'Leftinant Saahab...!' Chhagan Dubey yelled, his voice hoarse with excitement.

His finger was pointing towards someone far away, as he screamed again – this time his face flush with obvious glee and the rush of sudden, arrogant confidence.

'Leftinant Saahab... MASTAAAAAAAAAN...!!!'

The Old Fox

Delhi, December 1856

'Good morning, *Jahanpanaah*,' said Simon Fraser, as he stood up from his seat to welcome the old Mughal.

The Resident Commissioner of Delhi had to silently admit that even at his near-senile age, the Badshah of Hindustan looked strikingly regal. He lumbered in to the still-lavish *Diwan-e-Khaas* – the supremely regal meeting room reserved for the Emperor's select visitors, senior courtiers and choicest noblemen. Weighed down under his fabulous gold-brocaded gown and his royal pearls and jewels, Zafar was a painful ruin of what his ancestors had once been.

One could view Bahadur Shah as a dark-skinned, aging, frail and powerless old poet, surviving only on the crumbs that fell off the creaking relic of his dynastical table.

And yet, another could see him as who he really was - an ambitious monarch, a proud emperor, a seething heart and a ravaged soul. An old fox waiting patiently for his turn to pounce on the juiciest game ever hunted in world-history.

The wealth and populace of Hindustan!

'*As-salaamu Alaikum*, Badshah *salaamat*. You look healthy and well.'

'*Alhamdulillah. Wa-Alaikum-Assalaam*, Resident saahab' said the Mughal, smiling gently at the man he hated more than his blue soul could bear.

Just like his cold and surgical predecessor, Thomas Metcalfe, Fraser played along with the usual, farcical cycle of pleasantries. He knew who was in full and absolute control of this meeting. In control of Delhi. And in control of entire Hindustan.

'The East India Company submits its salutations and its allegiance, your royal Highness,' began the plump, wily old British officer.

'*Shukriya...*' mumbled Bahadur Shah, waving his bead-twirling fingers mystically like a *sufi* saint, trying desperately to hide his loathing and his disgust.

'Your Highness, there is something of concern that I need to discuss with you, with your permission, of course, Sire.'

'Go on, Resident saahab...'

Fraser now straightened his ornate tunic, kept his white busby on the ivory-clad table in front of him and came straight to the point.

'Your Highness, the young royal prince, Mirza Jawan Bakht, needs to be counseled. Much as he has inherited your divine grace and your boundless poise, his unbridled youth gets the better of him at times. We have been receiving several complaints and escalations, your Highness.'

For a moment, the Resident felt that Zafar had not even heard what he had said. But then he remembered all his previous audiences with the old Timurid.

The old scoundrel hears everything.

Several minutes passed as Fraser informed the old Mughal about the inappropriate conduct of the Badshah's favorite son – someone the king had wanted declared as his heir-apparent and had been canvassing for with the East India Company for years. But much to Zafar's now almost gangrenous consternation, first Thomas Metcalfe and now his successor Simon Fraser, both had persistently and steadfastly refused the Emperor this request.

After everything that they had slowly yet systematically snatched away from the wounded Timurid, this was the last straw on the old king's stooping back.

Ever since Bahadur Shah had ascended the cold and thorny throne of Delhi in 1837, not a week had passed without his authority and his stature being ruthlessly stripped away by the then Resident of Delhi, Thomas Metcalfe. After the demise of the icy and calculative Metcalfe, whispered by many in Delhi as nothing but a murder by slow-poisoning – handiwork of the Palace – the policy of undermining the throne of Delhi continued unabated under Metcalfe's successor, Simon Fraser.

Coins were no longer being minted in the Mughal's name. He was prohibited from bestowing titles and honors upon visiting *Rajas* and *Nawabs* of the princely states of Hindustan. His pension was being squeezed and he was not permitted to take decisions about his own crown jewels. Hailing from a dynasty that was once undoubtedly the master of the world's most fabulous riches, Zafar had been reduced to borrowing money from the money-lenders of Delhi. And with the East India Company's refusal to place his chosen son on the throne, the old Mughal's humiliation was complete.

His heart was now brimming over with scorching hate.

Bahadur Shah Zafar prayed every morning and every night for a chance at retribution.

Unbeknownst to him, his prayers were being heard.

Far-far away from Delhi, on the outskirts of the port of Calcutta, a rifle-cartridge manufacturing factory was forging bullets with the name of the East India Company written on them.

Mastaan

Delhi-Mathura Highway, December 1856

Robert D'Cruze turned to look in the direction that Chhagan Dubey was pointing towards.

The very next instant, the Lieutenant's ash and blood-stained face broke into a broad grin of reprieve and gratitude. What he beheld was a familiar sight – one that promised him a sure-shot gift, despite the day's horrible odds.

Yet again.

They were going to win the battle today.

In their typically impressive rifle-swirling move practiced over months and years, the riders of the incoming legion reloaded their guns with dazzling speed. Each of them used only one hand and their teeth to refill the smoking gun-barrels with black powder and round lead bullets. Even before the enemy could dive for cover, another volley of cartridges was fired by the incoming riders, almost each iron-pellet finding its mark.

Robert looked at these splendid men from his very own D'Cruze Regiment. In a flash, he remembered all the battles, that no one had believed were winnable, being won by this brilliant troop of warriors. Whether it was a fierce skirmish with the violent tribes of the eastern forests or a night-battle with the soldiers of powerful nawabs of the central provinces, the D'Cruze Regiment had built a reputation of being invincible.

Even though he was a full-blooded and fearless commander of his men himself, deep inside his heart Robert D'Cruze knew it was not his British leadership that had made his Regiment shine. Tales of the D'Cruze troops had travelled far and wide because of the man who was leading the incoming party of fifty formidable rifle-men.

The party was being led by the man every single one of them worshipped. These unafraid men were being led by who they believed was an unstoppable force of nature.

They were being led by the boisterous, flamboyant, loud-mouthed and magnificent...

Mastaan!

The Phaansigar felt as if they had been struck by a typhoon of whizzing bullets and scathing blades.

As the fifty riders of Mastaan's cavalry split into five columns, each devastating column charging into a different direction of the battlefield, they tore into the Thug formations. The first one to benefit from the dazzling onslaught of Mastaan himself was Subedaar-Major Chhagan.

As always, Chhagan was mesmerized when he saw Mastaan ride like the wind towards the manic Thugs that had surrounded his own tired Subedaar-Major self. Dressed in his typical flowing grey *mufti* outfit, galloping through the torrential rain atop a gleaming black stallion and twirling a menacing blade with his wrist, the approaching rider looked like a misty ethereal warrior from the fantasy tales. Moments before he pounced onto the horde of attackers surrounding Chhagan, Mastaan's feet were up on his saddle, as he rode his beauty of a mount without any grip on the reigns.

It was short work for the dreaded, brown-eyed, masterful fighter.

Wielding two short axes, one in each hand, Mastaan moved in, what could best be described as, a mingled blur of his long flowing hair, the gleam of his axe blades and the crimson shower from the gashed bodies of the Thugs. What was going to take Chhagan, if at all, forever, was accomplished by his inseparable friend Mastaan in a matter of a few seconds. Dead or dying Thugs now lay writhing all around Subedaar-Major Chhagan Dubey, with his friend kneeling in the center, in a battle stance, his arms outstretched and his axes dripping with Phaansigar blood.

In the midst of all the surrounding gunfire and slaughter, Chhagan could not help but quietly admire his childhood friend.

He was indeed magnificent.

Mastaan – the magnificent.

'Excuse me, Mastaan, you lout... why on earth are you interfering in my affairs?' shouted Chhagan at his friend. The Subedaar-Major was now panting with unhidden fatigue and respite.

Mastaan turned to look at Chhagan, with eyes sparkling like the north star, his handsome features accentuated under his youthful stubble and a thin film of sweat all over his face.

'I will deal with your blabbering a little later, Subedaar-Major saahab. For now, would you care to join me in rushing to Robert saab's aid?'

Chhagan nodded almost imperceptibly. Without a moment's delay he had picked up his sword and his dagger back in his firm grip.

After this quick exchange, both men scrambled towards the spot where Robert D'Cruze still fought valiantly against five bloodthirsty Thugs.

The remaining Phaansigar clambered frantically for cover.

Clawing their way through the wet mud in a failing endeavor to find some shelter behind bushes or tree trunks, by now, they had accepted the swift turn of fortunes.

But despite their desperate attempts to flee, each one of them was now being dragged back onto the battlefield, kicked with heavy service boots and hacked to pieces.

Mercilessly.

Under the righteous command of Lieutenant Robert D'Cruze, Subedaar-Major Chhagan Dubey and Subedaar Mastaan, the D'Cruze Regiment fought with great honor. Never was an unarmed adversary assaulted. Never did they harm a surrendering prisoner of war. Not once did the Regiment inflict damage on women and children. They never looted. Never raped. Never plundered. Never attacked a religious building. Never burnt homes or poisoned wells.

And it was for this distinguished service that his Company superiors had granted young Robert D'Cruze the exceptional honor of leading an entire Regiment ensigned under his own family name.

However, the Regiment charred all books of honor to ashes and buried all traces of humanity when confronted with those who ambushed and butchered their comrades in a cowardly fashion. Attacking from hidden rat-holes and murdering their brothers of the Regiment by surrounding them like the hyena, the Phaansigar had done themselves great disservice.

They were now paying the price for it.

The forest lair of the Thugs was being rinsed with Thug-blood.

It had taken Mastaan and Chhagan less than a few seconds to overpower the bandits besieging their Lieutenant.

'Ask your men to stop this massacre now, Mastaan,' said Robert. 'Arrest these dogs. Stop the killing! We are not them.'

'Yes, leftinant saahab,' replied Mastaan, as he threw his shoulder-length hair back, tying it into a loose pony-tail and blew a loud and sharp whistle that his men were fully familiar with. The killing stopped that very instant.

'But with your permission, *janaab*, may I ask the men to kill this Subedaar-Major Chhagnu? He is a liability...'

The three splendid men laughed out wholeheartedly, as Chhagan made a half-hearted attempt to land a kick on Mastaan's backside. Robert thoroughly enjoyed the endless banter between his two ablest men. He knew they were like blood-brothers, even though Chhagan was Mastaan's superior in rank. The two men could die for each other.

Little did this remarkable trio know then.

That the history of Delhi awaited them... and that they were fated to write it with their blood.

Nausha Mian

Darya Ganj, Delhi, December 1856

'Don't be an idiot, Mastaan... we cannot afford this place,' protested Chhagan.

It was payday. Tens of thousands of sepoys of the East India Company were in an upbeat mood. Unlike the ragtag, irregular and almost perpetually unpaid armies that the princes and nawabs of Hindustan maintained, the soldiers of the East India Company enjoyed a significantly more organized employment. Wages were paid regularly, allowances for uniforms were provided, rations were wholesome and dark rum was not a rarity.

And yet, something was not right.

There was anger seething as an undercurrent. The bond of trust that once knit the British officers and the Hindustani sepoys of the Company together into a formidable military behemoth, one that had conquered the entire sub-continent, had rapidly corroded with the passage of time and the rising might of the trading company.

'Don't be a miser, Chhagnu. Your beloved beauty from the *haveli* on the hill is not going to wait for you. Very soon she will marry a fat, bald Muslim merchant. So, no point saving money for her. We deserve the good life, my friend!' replied Mastaan, dragging his friend into *Sherbet*, the most expensive of Delhi taverns located in the elite streets of Darya Ganj – the residential area of the rich and powerful of the Mughal capital.

On this cold and foggy winter evening, Delhi sparkled like a queen's jewel. While it was well past its golden prime in the aftermath of Nadir Shah's bloodstained invasion and infamous *qatl-e-aam* or genocide in 1739, the relics of Delhi's glory were still unmatched by any other city in the world.

Even though the Mughal Badshah was caged in his own crumbling palace, the streets of Delhi teased the beholder like the timeless beauty of an aging harlot. The fragrance of the spices, the glitter of the *chudi* stalls, the street-side *mushairas* or poet congregations, the jingling of *paayal* from the courtesans' quarters, the aroma of roasting kebabs over slow fires... all of this blended exquisitely with Delhi's rich and intricate dialect. Every word spoken in the by-lanes of the greatest city of Hindustan was laced with the finesse of its unique *Ganga-Jamuni tehzeeb*. Delhi was beyond question what its residents believed it to be.

Dilli was *firdaus*.

It was paradise.

'But Mastaan, every pitcher of beer here is worth four paisa, brother. The way we drink, we will end up burning away a week's wages! This place is for the nobles, *bhai*. Let us go to

Sitara's tavern like we always do. I know you love the way she looks at you!'

Chhagan Dubey was trying his best to persuade his friend away from the sophisticated watering hole. He knew he was himself going to glug down two pitchers... at the very least. Mastaan would not stop before downing three or four! This ridiculous plan meant lighting several days' hard-earned salary with a match.

'One more pitcher!' screamed Chhagan, as he slammed his glass down on the polished wooden table of Sherbet, by now raising a few noblemen's eyebrows with his somewhat uncouth conduct. Its air fragranced with the expensive *ittra* of its patrons, Sherbet was a place that otherwise boasted of the most refined gentlemen from the famous high-streets and mansions of Delhi.

As the gorgeous waitress served Chhagan his fifth pitcher, she winked at the ruggedly handsome Mastaan. To her delight, he winked back. With all his masculine confidence bordering shamelessly on arrogance, this young man from *Oudh* (Awadh or modern-day Lucknow) thoroughly enjoyed his own magnetic charm when it came to the ladies. He was impudently flirtatious. And yet, somehow, he turned endearingly shy when at the receiving end of a bold woman's direct glare.

'Look, Mastaan... we all love Robert saahab. He is a gem of a man, no doubt. But things are changing, my friend. Something horrible seems to be lurking towards all of us... towards all of Dilli.'

Even in his drunk state, Subedaar-Major Chhagan Dubey was trying to say something to his closest friend.

'Chhagnu... don't scramble my brain and make...'

Even before Mastaan could complete his sentence, a loud table of aging noblemen erupted in praise for the gilded words of someone who appeared to be an audaciously conceited *shaayar* (poet).

'Baazicha-e-atfaal hai, duniya mere aagey;

Hota hai shab-o-roz tamasha mere aagey.'

'The world is nothing more than a playground of children for me;

Each day is all but a new theatrical drama played out for me.'

Both Mastaan and Chhagan turned to the table that seemed to be crowded with admirers of the aging poet.

The bearded, aged yet unconventionally striking shaayar continued.

'Matt poochh ke kya haal hai, mera tere peechhe;

Tu dekh ke kya rang hai, tera mere aagey.'

'Don't ask me what state I am in when you are not with me;

Observe what you become when you present yourself to be beholden by me.'

'Waah! Waah, Nausha Mian...! Mashallah!' the tavern erupted with thundering applause.

This poet from Delhi was indeed extraordinary.

Mastaan, who understood and appreciated a good Urdu couplet when he heard one, was instantly impressed. Such condescension, such unabashed immodesty in words... it was rare, brilliant! The poet's boldness directly matched the pride that the D'Cruze Regiment's most legendary warrior took in himself. He connected and identified with the old shaayar's *kalaam* immediately.

But Chhagan did not allow Mastaan to focus any further on the poetry.

He had something to warn his friend about. Something that was going to give an ominous new meaning to the name of the spectacular Mughal castle, in and around which the splendid city of Delhi was spread out.

Laal Qila.

The *Red Fort.*

The East India Company

Darya Ganj, Delhi, December 1856

'The sipahi are angry, Mastaan. All of them. You are blind if you cannot see it all around you!'

By now Chhagan was nearly completely inebriated. It was, in fact, the liquor that was giving him the courage to speak against the East India Company in front of his dearest friend – who was undoubtedly among the most loyal servants to the imperialistic trading giant.

Over barely a couple of centuries, the British East India Company had metamorphosed from being a humble trading outfit that paid taxes and homage to the Mughal court, into a mammoth political monster that dominated large swathes of Hindustan. With the defeat and cruel killing of someone widely believed to be invincible, the Tiger of Mysore Tipu Sultan, on 4th May, 1799, the Company became unstoppable. With this unquestioned military supremacy came the series of events that were to script the violent history of Hindustan over the next few decades – and lead to the bloodiest military uprising against British imperialism anywhere in the world.

The first few generations of English officers, clerks and soldiers who boarded creaking ships and arrived on the busy ports of Bombay and Calcutta during the early years of the trading company, fell in love with the Hindustan they discovered. The drastic change from the cold moors of the English countryside to the inviting, sunny plains of the Central Provinces – India was a welcome paradise.

From the lavishly embroidered native clothing to the dusky, beautiful Indian women, these Englishmen embraced the country with open arms. Exemplified by senior officers of the Company like Sir David Ochterlony, who began to dress like a Mughal nobleman and took thirteen Indian wives, the Englishmen unabashedly colored themselves in the rich palate of Indian culture. Several British officers took deep interest in the religious epics, philosophies and scriptures of Hindustan. Many of them enjoyed the hospitality of native friends and reciprocated in the same manner, relishing steaming kebabs and smoking the *hukkah* with great merriment. Innumerable British officers and soldiers settled down with their beloved Indian wives and nurtured offspring and happy households.

But then things changed, like they always do when one friend prospers orbits beyond the other. Unlike the strapping, impressionable young men that the Company sent to India in its early years, the new wave of Company officers came in at older ages, and with the conceited air of rulers, brimming with disdain for everything native.

Indians were not friends anymore. They were merely subjects. Hindustan was no more a land of wonder, soul-seeking and fantasy. It was a market ready to be exploited, offering fragmented kingdoms ready to be ruled. An aging Badshah, presiding over a dying dynasty, ripe to be thrown into the dustbins of history. Hindustani sepoys, once the greatest military asset of the Company, were now being taken for granted. A Company that was for long respected as an institution of enterprise, fairness and industry, had an entire continent rudely disillusioned when the nefarious Opium War was imposed upon China in the year 1839 and won.

Things worsened thereafter. The savage, unjustified annexation of Oudh earlier that year in February of 1856 made matters worse. Just like the kingdoms of Satara and Jhansi before it, the prosperous and culturally splendid kingdom of Oudh was wrested away from Nawab Wajid Ali Shah under Lord Dalhousie's draconian Doctrine of Lapse, and the pretext that the king of Oudh was a sexual debauch. All of Hindustan was stunned into anger at this ruthless injustice and glaring misuse of military supremacy.

Drunk with power, the East India Company had made more enemies than it could have ever envisaged.

And by far the most dangerous among these invisible enemies resided in the Company's own *chhaavanis* or cantonments. Hate had begun to simmer within the ranks of the Indian sepoys. Silent nods and glances among them were a telling sign of an impending, brutal uprising.

A great mutiny.

A battle to overthrow the yoke of a foreign oppressor.

A war for the unification and independence of all of Hindustan.

'Soch-samajh ke bol, Chhagnu...' warned an alarmed Mastaan. 'Think well before you speak, Chhagnu...'

For Mastaan the Company meant everything. It was not just his employer. It was his family. It was all he had.

His father, the late sipahi Ram Narayan Pandey, had been killed in service for the East India Company. Without hesitating for a moment, sipahi Pandey had covered the mouth of a flaming enemy cannon with his own body – in order to protect his British masters. They never found even a pound of his flesh to cremate as per Hindu rites.

As a conscientious repayment of this great debt, none other than the legendary William Fraser had taken in an orphaned Mastaan. Sipahi Pandey's boy had been raised by the formidable Englishman like his own son.

William Fraser, Agent to the Governor General of India and also the Commissioner of the Delhi Region, was a phenomenally domineering personality. A man who enjoyed hunting tigers armed with nothing but a spear, Fraser had embraced Mastaan and had personally taught the beautiful lad everything – shooting, hunting, riding, fighting with swords and spears, politics, Indian scriptures, appreciation for Urdu, for English and for art. He had leveraged the boy's unusual penchant for physical training and unarmed combat and had turned Mastaan into a fighting machine. It was not long before Fraser had realized that he was mentoring a child extraordinaire, a rare prodigy.

But once again destiny had a very different plan for Mastaan. As he turned barely ten years of age, following the footsteps of sipahi Ram Narayan Pandey, Fraser also left the young boy in an untimely fashion. On 22nd March 1835, the Commissioner of Delhi fell to an assassin's bullet on the hill of the Delhi Ridge. Orphaned again, Mastaan soon found himself lodged in the sweaty barracks of the Company's cantonments. But by this time Fraser had ensured two things. One, that loyalty to the East India Company ran in the very bloodstream of Mastaan's body.

And two, that sipahi Pandey's son was set to emerge as all of Hindustan's greatest combat soldier.

Mohalla Ballimaran

Darya Ganj, Delhi, December 1856

Mastaan bundled his drunk friend into a hired palanquin. His dear Chhagnu had passed out, mumbling something that was disturbing Mastaan deeply. His words against the *Company Bahadur*, as the East India Company was commonly referred to in India, were ringing in the ears of William Fraser's protégé.

'Everyone is angry, Mastaan...' Chhagan had said in his slurring yet well-meaning gabble.

'The Company Bahadur now treats us like animals. It is not the same as it was in the days of Fraser saahab or the other benevolent officers of the good old times. Mark my words, Mastaan... a revolt is going to raise its ugly head against the Company any day now. You know the officers well, Mastaan... they respect you more than any of us... you speak their language. Talk to them... warn them... my friend...'

As Chhagan's palanquin disappeared into a narrow lane of the Mughal city, Mastaan turned to walk towards the Company chhaavani all by himself. Worried as he was, he enjoyed these solo, long walks in the constricted by-lanes of the city - that eventually merged into the sparkling high-streets of *Chandni Chowk* or into the windy banks of the Jumna (Yamuna) river on the far side.

While it was well past midnight, the vibrant city of Delhi had not turned-in for the night. Many a *maikhaana* or wine-bar was open even now, catering to the revelers for whom the evening had just begun. The air of the glowing city was rich with the aromas of scented wines, charcoal grilled spiced meats and the fragrance of jasmine emanating from the *gajra* of the intoxicating Delhi courtesans, or from the wrists of their most intimate guests.

The night was far from quiet. The melodious jingling of dancers' paayals blended with the sound of soul-searching *ghazal* recitals, or the distant rhythmic percussion of the *tabla*. Mastaan smiled to himself.

This city is blessed by the Gods.

As he crossed the imposing *Jama Masjid* from a distance and the *Kabutar Bazaar* (pigeon market) to his left, Mastaan saw an old man in a big gown and a tall Turkish cap doubled-up over an open drain, holding on to a wall's edge to maintain his precarious balance. Mastaan figured that the senile nobleman was totally drunk.

Mastaan was not one to leave an old man unattended, even if the timeworn gentleman had inflicted his current state upon himself by excessive consumption of what was, as Mastaan's olfactory senses could tell, rose-scented wine.

How many drunk men do I need to tend to tonight?!

'May I help you, Sir...?' asked Mastaan, bending a little to enable the old drunk to see him.

In a flash, the Subedaar of D'Cruze Regiment recognized the intoxicated man's face.

The conceited shaayar from the tavern!

'Thank you... but no thank you, young man! Go on... go on along your path. Let none among us pretend as if we live anymore in the gracious Delhi of yore,' replied the old poet, laughing cynically and coughing at the same time.

Mastaan did not flinch, even as he empathized with the painful plea in the aging poet's words. All of Delhi's old timers today shared this common lament. Without hesitating Mastaan took hold of the shaayar's elbow and gently raised the man's arm around his own shoulder. He wrapped his other arm around the poet's waist and assisted him to stand straight and start walking.

'I will drop you home, Sir. Where do you live?'

Even in his drunk state, the arrogant shaayar from Sherbet turned to look at Mastaan. He had the most intelligent and piercing eyes Mastaan had ever seen in a man so advanced in age.

'Drop me to Ballimaran, if you must...' the old man stuttered, still showing absolutely no sign of reduced smugness.

'Ballimaran?' exclaimed an excited Mastaan. 'That is the *mohalla* (neighborhood) where even the great Mirza Asadullah Baig Khan also lives! You must be knowing him...?'

'Hah! You know of him...?'

'Yes, of course! Who doesn't know of the greatest shaayar of modern times? I have never seen him, but I follow his work. He is absolutely brilliant... don't you think?'

The old poet in the Turkish hat laughed out loud, once again his laughter ending with a violent bout of coughing.

'Hmmm... he is just about okay.'

'Why did you say let us not pretend that we live in the Delhi of yore, Sir?' asked Mastaan, as the two of them trudged along the now dimming streets towards the colony of Ballimaran. 'And why was everyone at Sherbet addressing you as Nausha Mian? As I understand, Nausha means a groom or a son-in-law...'

The poet grinned and nodded. There was definitely something extraordinary about this man, Mastaan thought.

'Let me answer your second question first, young man... what did you say your name was?'

'They call me Mastaan, *bade mian*.'

'Mastaan? But you don't seem to be a *Mussalmaan*, my friend. Mastaan is a Persian name, meaning one who is intoxicated in the elixir of God. So, what is your story?'

William Fraser's protégé smiled and replied, keeping his answer as brief as possible.

'I was named by a very generous Englishman. He named me after the scimitar of a great Persian king. Apparently, the legendary sword called Mastaan never lost a battle.'

'Hmm... a sword? Impressive. And true to your name, with your long tresses, those deep eyes and your lean muscular built, you must be quite the slayer among the incomparable beauties of Delhi!' exclaimed the drunk old man laughing, suddenly sounding a lot less drunk.

'You know, Mastaan,' the aging shaayar continued, 'the Delhi your young eyes witness today is just a bleak patch on the paradise city it once was. When I got married and came here to live with my in-laws from my hometown of Agra, hence the name Nausha Mian by the way, I felt as if I had entered the doors of heaven, the gates of *jannat*. But just like the most divine and pious among beauties draw vile stares of the most decadent of men, the fragrance of this city of cities became irresistible for the men who were overcome with lust – for wealth, for conquest and for overlord-ship. They came and tore this beauty to shreds, murdered her lovers and burnt down the homes and temples that held her in boundless adoration. And look what we have become today. The noblemen of this day have the manners and courtesies like those of the cup-bearers of Delhi in its golden age. The poets that adorn the tired court of the Great Mughals today are equal in talent to that of the palanquin-bearers of the Delhi of yore!'

With these grieving words of evident dejection, the old shaayar raised his arm to indicate that they had arrived at his destination.

The mohalla of Ballimaran.

'You can stop here, young man. We have reached the *gareebkhana*, the humble abode of yours truly.'

Something magnetic about the inebriated shaayar set him apart from all the other noblemen and poets of Delhi that Mastaan had had the opportunity of meeting.

As the tired old man tapped the young warrior's shoulder in a subtle yet affectionate expression of gratitude and turned to leave, Mastaan felt the urge to meet this unusually intelligent, strangely inspiring man again.

'Nausha Mian... you did not tell me your name. My friend and I heard your verses at the tavern in Darya Ganj. They were out of this world! What is your name, bade mian, and what is your pen-name?' Mastaan called out.

The shaayar wrapped his flowing robe tightly around himself to fight off the biting cold. He turned and smiled at Mastaan, raised his hand in slow farewell, as he uttered another sher before disappearing behind the *purdah* that guarded the pride of his dilapidated *haveli*.

'Haiin aur bhi zamaane mein sukhanvar bahaut achhe;

Kehte haiin ke Ghalib ka hai, andaaz-e-bayaan aur.'

'While there are several other excellent poets in the world;

They say that Ghalib has a class of expression altogether superior.'

For several moments Mastaan stood dumbstruck at the entrance of this ill-maintained haveli. It was only now that it struck him.

How could I have been such a fool?

I have just dropped home a legendary shaayar – the most immortal of them all!

Mastaan turned around, slapped his head in joyous rebuke and laughed as he walked away from the small haveli in Ballimaran.

Good night, Mirza Nausha, he thought to himself.

Good night, Mirza Ghalib.

The Half-Faced Dervish

Underbelly of the Red Fort, Delhi, December 1856

The stench of rotting corpses was unmistakable.

That such a chamber of horrors existed right below the ramparts of the Laal Qila was known only to the Badshah, to his select few loyalists... and to the dark dervishes of Delhi.

Dervish is a term that mostly means a Sufi saint, a man of God. Dervishes appeared in the streets of Delhi and large parts of northern Hindustan during the 12th century. A dervish could be spotted from a distance – singing, dancing, howling, twirling his head, rolling up his eyes, surrounded by incense smoke. They blessed all those who came their way. Welcome guests at weddings and other holy ceremonies, they were known to cure illnesses, heal the grievously wounded and banish evil spirits from homes of the faithful. Some believed that dervishes spoke straight to the angels in heaven. Others were convinced that they controlled powerful and terrifying *djinns*, unearthly beings that haunted the old castles and havelis of Delhi.

However, what many did not know was that one section of dervishes comprised practitioners of the black arts. From summoning the *rooh* or spirits of the dead to performing the worship of *Shaitaan* or Satan, these dangerous mystics delved into the ethereal and forbidden realms.

Zafar could sense both fear and gnawing guilt creeping deep inside the recesses of his rapidly degenerating soul. He knew what he was there for. The cavern of the half-faced dervish was no place for the pious, the good-hearted or the faithful. It was the last refuge for those who were willing to strike a deal with the overlord of the dark dominions. It was the violating, unnatural crossover bridge for those willing to become ghosts even while they lived – their souls plucked out by the ghoulish claws of shaitaan.

The dark forces that emanated from the underworld at the behest of this ghastly, powerful dervish, indeed granted the desperate petitioners what they wished for – albeit each time with a tragic and cruel twist. And that was not all. The otherworldly forces invariably extracted a horrific, unspeakable price in return - a bargain that was unveiled only when the despairing seeker had gone far ahead into the terrifying path.

Too far.

The glow of the humid underground chamber was an eerie blue. Something conjured by the half-faced dervish had an ominous effect on even the simple phenomena of nature. Fire torches that normally glowed a bright yellow, turning dark spaces amber, now glimmered in a haunting bluish-green. The concealed cave, the lair of the half-faced dervish, was connected via a serpentine underground canal to the Yamuna, and the waters of the great river flowed into this evil burrow. The reflection of the blue-flamed torches fell on the mildly choppy waves, that clapped against the rocky walls and reflected the blue light oddly all around the cavern.

And there he sat... huddled into himself, rising like a murky shadow on a stone platform next to the inky blue water...

...the most terrifying black-magician of Delhi.

A man most people believed to be nothing more than a dark legend. Others were convinced that he had long died a slow and painful death, buried alive decades ago.

But here he was.

The half-faced dervish!

Zafar bit his lip, gripped by fear, as the dark dervish turned to look at the Emperor. It was a sight that could stop the beating heart of even a young lion.

The dervish's face was horrifying. It was by far the ugliest, the most evil and undoubtedly the most repulsive human face on the planet. In fact, it was hard to say whether it was human at all. It seemed like there were two of them. One half of his face was old, wrinkled and leathery as if he were two hundred years old. But it was the other half that terrified and froze the soul. The other side of the dervish's face seemed like its skin and a layer of flesh had been mercilessly torn away. His fully visible globular eyeball danced around amidst this monstrous melt of bone, muscle and blood.

As he saw Zafar's face contort with terror and disgust, the dervish gazed deep into the king's eyes.

He then wobbled his head from side to side, like he was done reading Zafar's mind and had peered into the old king's soul. He then hissed a few words, as if speaking to someone far-far away... to someone from another world.

'Greed, ambition... beyond all measure...;

The soft hearts died... with Tipu's treasure...!'

Reciting this mysterious limerick, the dervish began to guffaw like a goblin, his wicked laughter filling up the evil dank cave like the laugh of a hundred djinns combined.

A Letter from Meerut

Mohalla Churi Walan, Delhi, December 1856

It was the best time of the day.

Late winter mornings on the low-rise terraces of the congested but colorful housing colonies surrounding the imposing domes of the magnificent Jama Masjid, were luxurious hours that made this frosty season of Delhi inspire many a work of romance.

The winters of Delhi, like many poetic old-timers of the city maintained, made every finer aspect of living significantly better. From the pleasures of love-making under the lukewarm glow of a lantern on cold foggy nights, to the amorous longing of a forlorn lover waiting by the riverbank in the winter mist; from the unmatched taste of goat meat that melted in the mouth, to the crunchy flavors of Afghani *pistas* washed down with the finest wines and beers - as one basked in the golden glow of the afternoon Sun. This bliss was an exclusive gift from the heavens to *Dilli-wallahs* alone.

As thousands of pigeons flew out into the blue skies from the roof-top patios of nearly every house in the *galli* Churi Walan, there was one man who partook in none of the delightful sunny activities.

Subedaar-Major Chhagan Dubey sat with his head clutched in his hands, nursing a terrible hangover. The fact that he had also made his own purse much lighter at Sherbet the evening before was not helping. And the incessant snickering and teasing from Mastaan and two other friends from the D'Cruze Regiment were only compounding the man's suffering.

'They say one should never stretch one's legs beyond the length of one's blanket, Mastaan...' remarked Balram Rai, a veteran *sawaar* or horseman of the D'Cruze Regiment. He could barely hold back his good-hearted laughter.

'Yes... yes... I agree...' quipped Shahbaaz, another rider from the D'Cruze troopers, a good friend of Mastaan and Chhagan. 'One must save for the rainy day...'

Mastaan was observing Chhagan's reactions from the corner of his eye. He could tell there was still some room for more leg-pulling.

'Especially when one is in love, *yaar* Shahbaaz,' added Mastaan. 'That too when it is with a rich maiden from the hilltop bungalow. Chhagnu and *Majnu* rhyme somewhat, do they not?'

'WILL YOU GUYS PLEASE SHUT UP?!' erupted Chhagan, suddenly and uncharacteristically. His eyes were ablaze as he looked up.

While the trio of sawaar Balram, sawaar Shahbaaz and Subedaar Mastaan knew they were pushing the Subedaar-

Major a little too much this morning, none of them expected such a violent response.

Something more than just a hangover and a spending spree was on the Subedaar-Major's mind.

Something a lot more worrisome.

'What happened there, Chhagnu...?' asked Mastaan, as he applied generous amounts of mustard oil to his own long tresses, muscular shoulders and arms.

They were now away from the others, seated on the terrace parapet of the house of Chhagan's parents. Chhagan's sister, the bubbly 19-year-old Sujata, served them some hot ginger tea.

'Thank you, *bitiya*,' said Mastaan, as he brushed her head with his palm, in a gesture of affectionate blessing.

'What's wrong with Chhagan bhaiya, Mastaan dada?' asked Sujata, her eyes twinkling with naughtiness. 'Is it that Muslim girl again?'

Chhagan turned and glared at her in anger.

Mastaan tried to control his laughter, raised his finger to his lips, indicating to Sujata that the Subedaar-Major was not in a humorous mood.

Sujata widened her eyes, bit her tongue and left with a mischievous giggle.

After a minute, Mastaan asked again.

'*Bataa na*, Chhagnu... what is the matter?'

The Subedaar-Major did not respond. He seemed to be looking far away into the horizon, lost in thought. From what Mastaan could sense, these were not happy thoughts.

'You know, Mastaan,' began Chhagan finally, 'there is more to life than just cutting down enemies with our swords, drinking heavily at taverns, laughing our guts out as if nothing around mattered – and blindly following the orders of the Company Bahadur like we were nothing more than sheep.'

The long-haired Subedaar's oil-smeared hands stopped where they were. He raised his eyebrows and stared at Chhagan, not hiding his displeasure or admonition. This was the second time in twenty-four hours that his dearest friend and D'Cruze Regiment superior had expressed resentment against the Company Bahadur. Only this time Chhagan was not even drunk.

The Subedaar-Major continued, nonetheless.

'We are not children anymore, Mastaan. Nor are we some eighteen-year-olds who can remain blissfully unaware of our surroundings. Can you not see which side the wind blows, my friend? The East India Company has changed. Its officers have changed! We are no more the brothers-in-arms we used to be with our commanders once. We are just fighting corpses for them... nameless, faceless riflemen. In any case, the Company Bahadur is now recruiting more and more Gurkhas and Sikhs. After all these decades of service and blood that we have offered to the *firangis*, they trust the Gurkhas and Sikhs more now than...'

'Chhagnu... stop it! Have you lost your mind?' exclaimed Mastaan, interrupting his friend, his eyes wide with disbelief.

Among other things, this was the first time he had heard the derogatory term *firangi* from Chhagan's mouth.

'If anyone hears a word of what you are saying, Chhagnu, you well know what the consequences will be! They will charge you with treason, and although they will never be able to execute the punishment while I am still alive, you *will* be condemned to the gallows! What has come over you, Dubey? We are loyal servants of the Company Bahadur. We live and die for the East India Company!'

'No, we don't, Mastaan! No, we don't... not anymore!' retorted Chhagan, throwing his earthen cup of tea crashing into the rough brick floor of the terrace.

The two friends sat in silence for a couple of minutes, both breathing heavily with anger, both jostling with the storms brewing in their minds. It was the Subedaar-Major who spoke first.

'Look, Mastaan... I know everything that William Fraser saahab did for you. We all remember him from our childhood. What a man he was... what a lion! He had the heart of a king and the generosity of a loving father. But where are officers like William Fraser today, bhai? Do they even eat a meal with us, let alone inviting us to their homes? Do they marry Indian women anymore? Why do they have so much disdain for native clothing? Why are they humiliating the Mughal

Emperor so brazenly? Why have they usurped Jhansi? And Satara? And even your own Awadh, Mastaan? You yourself dislike that Padre Jennings so much. You know he is out to destroy both Hindus and Mussalmaans of Delhi, and to convert them to Christianity. Why is the Company Bahadur encouraging him? Why do they want to destroy our religions? The newly enrolled sipahis are being asked to take ships to fight wars several oceans away. Don't the commanders of the Company Bahadur know such travel is forbidden for us Hindus? Do you not see, my brother... they want to annex and rule all of Hindustan? They are out to destroy our beliefs, our heritage and our way of life!'

With every word that Chhagan spoke, Mastaan felt a chill go down his spine. He knew what the East India Company did with mutineers. He knew about the vast spy network that reported into the Company Bahadur. He was certain that it would not be long before Chhagnu was caught, tried and condemned to be hanged. But above everything else, he was stunned to see a loyal soldier of the British speaking against his own masters so audaciously.

'Chhagnu, you have got to stop this talk right now and promise never to repeat it again. We have sworn loyalty to the Company Bahadur. We eat their salt! Even if you are right about a majority of the Englishmen, we still have brave and just officers like Leftinant Robert leading us. Here on, you cannot trust anyone with such conversation, Subedaar-Major saahab.'

Chhagan was unmoved. From the hardened look on his friend's face, Mastaan could see his words were not hitting home. He pressed on.

'You are inviting the wrath of the entire British force, Chhagan. You, me, a handful of other soldiers... we cannot take on the might of the East India Company even if we wanted to. When the whole of China and powerful kingdoms with large armies could not stand up to them, who on earth do you think we are? Even the mighty Tipu Sultan could not fight them, Chhagnu. They say the Company Bahadur has crushed even the *fraancisi* (French) back in Europe and Arabia. Battle after battle, their naval fleets have sunk the ships of all their adversaries. They are masters of the entire world, Chhagnu!'

'Yes, they are... but not for long! At least Hindustan will be free of their yolk very soon,' replied Chhagan Dubey, determinedly muttering the second half of his statement to himself.

Mastaan shook his head in fear and despair at the madness coming over his friend.

'And how do you plan to overthrow the Company Bahadur from Hindustan singlehandedly, may I ask, Dubey saahab?' he asked, his tone not hiding the sarcasm.

It was only now that the Subedaar-Major turned to look at his friend and smiled faintly. His eyes were gleaming. Mastaan did not like the look on his friend's face. It was not the look of a frontal warrior. In stark contrast with Chhagan's courageous, honest and kindhearted nature, it was the twisted expression of a conspirator planning to attack his enemy from behind.

'I am not alone, Subedaar saahab. I have received a letter,' said Chhagan, in nothing more than a whisper.

'What letter, Chhagnu?'

'It is a secret letter from the Subedaar-Major of the Meerut troops, Mastaan. It is from the 3rd Bengal Light Infantry stationed at the Meerut chhaavani.'

'What does it say? I don't like the look on your face or the tone of your voice. What have you not told me?'

Chhagan put his hand on Mastaan's shoulder and laughed an anxious, menacing laugh before uttering those foretelling but horribly incomplete words.

'The soldiers are uniting, my brother.

Very soon Delhi is going to drown in firangi blood.'

Laughs and laughs... the Tiger of Mysore!

Underbelly of the Red Fort, Delhi, December 1856

'Speak out your desires, Badshah...'

By now Zafar, along with his friend and physician Ahsanullah Khan, had spent several hours in the subterranean cavern, participating in the horrific black-magic rituals performed by the ghastly half-faced dervish.

Using his sickly thin hands, the ugly sorcerer had pierced and carved several rotting dead bodies with a long knife blackened with the soot of coal fires. Chanting unnerving gibberish in a language that resembled the most ancient form of Persian, he had completed grisly occult rituals on the unfortunate cadavers who had not found peace even in death. He drew bizarre figurines with their dried blood on the rock platform he sat on, before rolling them over into the water that appeared to be swallowing corpses like a slithering giant black python.

With each such horrific offering, the dervish seemed to be getting closer and closer to connecting with whatever evil power he was attempting to build an unearthly bridge towards. The last macabre rite was the mixing of Zafar's own thick blood with that of a cobra, and the sickening concoction was then poured into the black waters as a final offering. The section of the river under this dark chamber seemed to have been cut-off from the mainstream of the pious, lifegiving Jumna. This was outlandish water - black, viscous, lurking, hissing... and cursed.

It was the dark wizard's cauldron of horror.

'Speak out your desires, Badshah...' repeated the ghostly conjurer.

Bahadur Shah paused for a moment, took a deep breath and spelled out his dark yearnings one after the other... oblivious to the terrifying price he would soon have to pay in return.

'Grant me this wish, O dervish... that I, Bahadur Shah the second, command an army larger than even that of Timur the Lame!'

'*Graaaanted...* says the djinn of Seringapatam!' hissed the dervish almost instantly, rolling up his eyes diagonally, as if listening to someone far-far away.

'Ask for more, Badshah... ask for *mooore...*' he urged, his claw-like fingers rolling into his palms, as if he were pulling out the last remnants of the Emperor's goodness.

'Grant me this wish, O conjurer of the hidden spells... that the British... the heathen that have sucked the blood of all of Hindustan, are forced to fall to their knees and beg for mercy... before my eyes!'

Thus pronounced the old Mughal his second wish, himself unable to believe the words escaping his trembling lips.

This is not me!

'*Graaaanted!* The djinn says he grants this wish as well, O Badshah...' scowled the goblin of a man, now breaking into bursts of sinister laughter. His eyes, his black soul, his crooked fangs... were all mocking the hapless king of Delhi.

Except that the king of Delhi was unable to see any of it. He was now in a trance. His soul was in the merciless grip of a ghost...

Was it the undead spirit from the haunted fort of Mysore, fifteen hundred miles away?

Or a ghost lurking deep inside the Badshah's own troubled and deformed mind?

Who could tell?

'Ask for more... you still have one wish left... ask for *mooore*,' coaxed the dervish further.

The king's confidante, Ahsanullah Khan, who was witness to the ghastly proceedings, was now certain that Zafar was not in control of his words or of his actions anymore. The senile king's eyes were now entirely black, and he looked far older than what he actually was. His body was strangely twisted, his fingers unnaturally knotted and his head was tilted to one side. The king's trusted doctor, who was well-versed with the black arts of the dervishes, was now convinced that it was not Zafar in the body of the old man any more.

From what the old physician could tell, the Emperor was completely possessed by the powerful ethereal being that had been summoned to the cave of horrors by the half-faced magician.

'One more wish... you must ask for it, Badshah... AAASK!' snarled the black-magician with the half-skinned face.

'Do not ask for anything more, Jahanpanaah,' implored Ahsanullah, as he struggled to wrench his eyes away from the serpent-like glare of the dervish, to look into those of his king.

'This is not you, my lord... your eyes display the evil glint of the devil himself! Your voice sounds like the rasping growl of someone long dead! Your body is misshapen, O khalifa... this dervish is an imp of Shaitaan! Free yourself, my lord... let us flee this dungeon of the dead!'

But it was far too late for the Mughal monarch to turn back.

'Grant me this wish...' he began.

Even before the possessed Zafar could spell out what he was going to ask for, the half-faced ghoul cackled, with maddening glee.

Then he suddenly stopped laughing, looked at Ahsanullah in a derisive manner, and mouthed another inexplicable verse -

The haunted tomb's curse... rises to the fore...;

Laughs and laughs... the Tiger of Mysore...!

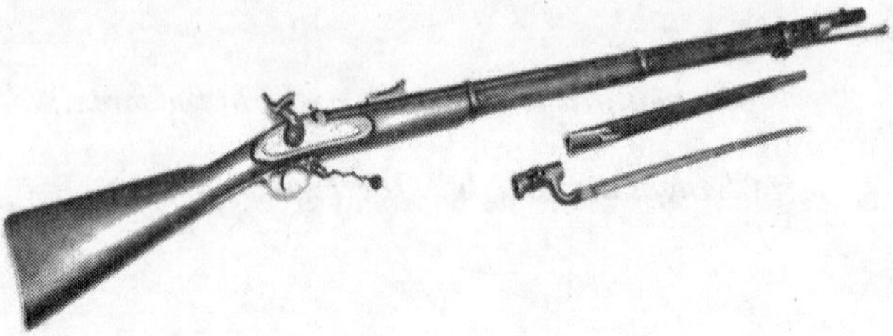

Enfield Rifles

Bara Hindu Rao, Delhi, February 1857

The two men rode all the way from the Delhi cantonment to the residence of their Regiment commander without a word exchanged between them. Several weeks had passed since their tense exchange on the terrace of Chhagan Dubey's ancestral home at Churi Walan.

Lieutenant Robert D'Cruze had sent for his two best men and was waiting at his modest yet well-appointed bungalow near Metcalfe House, the grand mansion built by the previous British Resident of Delhi, Sir Thomas Metcalfe. The imposing building was now the abode of his son Theophilus or better known as Theo. The sprawling palace of sorts had been built as a bold and unequivocal announcement by Thomas Metcalfe to indicate who the real master of Delhi was.

As they crossed the hilly and densely forested Delhi Ridge with the enormous house of the rich merchant Hindu Rao to their far right, Chhagan softened a little. He knew Mastaan silently grieved and relived the loss of his Godparent William Fraser every time he crossed this stretch. It was here, right at the Hindu Rao ridge, that Fraser had fallen victim to the carbine bullet of an assassin. It was William Fraser who had bought the grand Hindu Rao bungalow, as its second owner and resident. It was where Mastaan grew up.

'You alright, Mastaan...?'

The Subedaar nodded, looking straight ahead. While he did not express it as often as he would have liked to, deep down the friendship of Chhagan meant everything to the brilliant warrior. His Chhagnu was the only family he had. And it was the rising aversion between his inseparable friend and the Company he was fiercely devoted to that was keeping Mastaan awake at nights. He was well aware that Chhagan was not alone in his growing despise for the British. Murmurs of disaffection and even downright hatred could be heard from every corner of the chhaavani. Something really big and unimaginable seemed to be brewing in the undercurrents. What Mastaan found most disturbing was that the Company officials seemed to be totally and blissfully oblivious to what now seemed imminent.

A violent sepoy uprising.

He did not know where things were headed and how bad it could be. All he knew was that if there was a showdown one day and sides had to be picked, he would be faced with the hardest choice of his life. A clash between the East India Company and its own sepoys was going to ink a chapter so bloody that history would not be able to erase it from its memory till the end of time.

What Mastaan did not know as they rode past the Flagstaff Tower towards Metcalfe House - was that the day to pick sides was not far.

'At ease, gentlemen,' said Lieutenant D'Cruze responding to the smart salutes from Chhagan and Mastaan.

The young officer settled into his garden chair and, with a gesture from his hand, invited the two fine men to join him. Robert D'Cruze was among the handful of Englishmen who continued to treat their men with the respect the soldiers deserved.

Chhagan stepped forward, pulled back a chair and sat down. This was awkward for both Mastaan and Robert. While it was Robert's civility that made him break convention and offer the men a place at his table, none of the Hindustani soldiers ever availed of the opportunity. Such offers were always responded to with a smile and a *namaste*, and the men never took a seat in front of their officers. This was the unsaid show of courtesy from both sides.

But today was different.

Robert was taken aback for a moment or two at Chhagan's sudden and unexpected breach of their tacit and longstanding behavioral equation. Nonetheless, he ignored the mild audacity with an irritated twitch of the brow and went ahead with sharing what he had been mandated with by his superiors.

'There is news, gentlemen. The Company Bahadur has decided to upgrade the rifles of the D'Cruze Regiment. In fact, not just of the D'Cruze Regiment. Over the next few months, rifles of the entire infantry of the East India Company will be upgraded.'

Chhagan and Mastaan exchanged bewildered glances before the Subedaar-Major spoke. Despite his initial show of assertion, Chhagan's tone was cordial as ever. He admired Robert D'Cruze deeply.

'Why this change in our firearms, Robert saahab? Our guns are perfect, and we have spent years training our men on them. Mastaan's *paltan* is especially very proficient on these rifles and his men are extraordinary marksmen!'

'Yes, yes... I know what you are saying, Chhagan,' replied Robert patiently. 'But the new Pattern 1853 Enfield rifles that are being commissioned are much superior in performance to the Brown Bess muskets we use in the infantry currently. As I have been told by the ordnance engineers, the barrels of the new Enfield are grooved from the inside, which makes them significantly more lethal than the current issue of weapons.'

'That would not be a problem, Chhagan,' intervened Mastaan. 'I will train the men again. They are all ace marksmen by instinct. They will catch up with the Enfield rifles in no time. If these new guns are significantly more accurate and longer-range, this change will only make us more effective on the field of battle.'

'So, what are the orders, Sir?' asked Chhagan, after deliberating for a minute over the information shared by Lieutenant D'Cruze and the reassurance from Mastaan. More lethal rifles meant better chances of winning battles and lesser loss of life for the Subedaar-Major's men. Even if it meant a few months of extra training, the change sounded worthwhile.

'We have been ordered to shift base to Ambala, where the new rifles and cartridges will be issued to...'

Even as the Lieutenant was speaking, something happened that made all of Robert's remaining words fade away for Mastaan. Something beautiful... that was going to change the magnificent fighter's life forever.

Something fateful... that was going to alter the destiny of an entire nation.

Like a silver bolt of lightning had pierced through his heart. Like an *apsara* from the heavens had stepped onto the realm of the mortals. Like the blessings of the Gods had taken human shape...

...he saw *her*.

The most beautiful face he had ever beheld in his life.

The Lion of Peshawar

Frontier Tribal Area, Afghanistan Border, February 1857

He looked like an angry God from the ancient Greek myths.

As his towering figure emerged from his dusty tent in the Peshawar region of northwest Hindustan, the rugged and battle-hardened men of his notorious company roared in unison.

'Nikhaal-bhagwaan ki... JAI!'

Victory to the God Nikhaal!

The monster with gleaming black eyes like those of the messenger of death, standing nearly seven feet tall, snarled and turned to glower at his men like a dragon infuriated. He was known to order mindless whipping of his native soldiers every time they heralded him as a God.

It did not matter. The men, even at the cost of risking his brutal wrath, screamed again. Whether they worshipped him like a revered deity or feared him like a walking ghost, it was unclear. They seemed to be living and breathing under his spell.

'Nikhaal-bhagwaan ki... JAI!'

Given his superhuman strength, his bestial cruelty and his unfathomable combat-skills, this British warlord of sorts was the most dreaded name across the barren lands of Peshawar.

Brigadier General Jon Nicholson.

The sandstorm blew stronger as Nicholson walked the muddy path towards the makeshift arena made for him and the savage man who awaited him.

The northwest of Hindustan was among the most vicious and barbaric regions in the sub-continent. A land that everyone from the great Alexander of Macedon to the mighty Mongol Genghis Khan had attempted to invade, this beautiful yet desolate country had bloodshed and conflict inscribed on every speck of its golden sand.

The mountainous region of Peshawar and beyond was ruled by formidable warlords, each with his own private militia. Every growing lad, from the prompt age of eleven, carried deadly weapons in this bandit country, making it one of the most difficult territories to control and govern. And it was for this reason that none other than their very own God of violence, Brigadier General Nicholson, had been posted in Peshawar by the East India Company.

The arena had no real boundary except for the men of the Company's platoons surrounding it in a human ring. Thousands more watched from a distance, Afghan men and women, most of them perched on low nearby hills or on their fabulous horses. The man that kneeled in the middle of the dusty stadium of sorts had his hands tied behind his back. His head was bowed, and his bearded chin rested on his chest. His long hair was falling in front of his face, hiding it almost completely.

But this submissive posture was not even remotely an indication of the reality of this widely feared monster. The ferocity and madness of this bull of a man were known far and wide across the Hindukush foothills. In magnitude of his muscular built he was in no way inferior to the giant that was walking towards him.

After a long siege around his encampments in the mountainous terrain, the Company had finally succeeded in apprehending the most cruel and oppressive of all Afghan warlords.

The Lion of Peshawar.

Abu-Zar Pasha!

The laws of these tribal lands were as bizarre as they were barbarous. Only a man who could prove himself to be the most fearless and unbeatable among them, could hope to keep these warring tribes under some semblance of governance. They did not respect victories that involved outnumbering or outmaneuvering a warrior. They cared for no form of organized authority or sovereign symbol. Military superiority meant nothing to them.

When it came to the measure of a fighter, it was only what he could do alone that mattered.

As was the medieval custom in these lands, any man condemned to the death penalty had a last option that he could exercise. A condemned man could choose between the comparatively painless punishment of a clean beheading or an unarmed duel with his captor in full public view. The obvious caveat was that the captor had a right to refuse the second route.

However, most ferocious Afghan warlords embraced the second option chosen by their prisoners.

And Jon Nicholson was anyway not one to turn his back on a fight. Especially not when thousands of Pashtun tribesmen, who he was responsible to govern on behalf of the East India Company, were watching from the ringside.

He had accepted the fight-unto-death challenge from the terrifying Afghan, Abu-Zar Pasha.

The no-holds-barred, unarmed and savage battle between the Lion of Peshawar and the legendary white man, who the sepoys of the Company believed to be a God incarnated, was about to begin.

Fay

Near Metcalfe House, Delhi, February 1857

Mastaan froze as she walked towards them.

Her face was chiseled to perfection. Her fair skin glowed like shining ivory against the morning sun. She wore a flowing white dress with blue flowers and strode towards Lieutenant D'Cruze's table with a beatific smile and a confident twinkle in her eyes.

'Oh hullo, Fay! How is my little sister this morning?' greeted Robert cheerily, as the young girl came closer to where the men were sitting.

Fay.

Mastaan could not take his eyes away from her bewitchingly beautiful features.

Fay.

He kept repeating her name in his mind. His eyes were locked on her stunning face.

'Mastaan...'

Her blue eyes cannot be real. No one can be this lovely, this exquisite...

'Mastaaaaan...!' repeated Robert, this time in a raised voice.

'Err... yes... yes, Sir,' replied the brilliant battler of the D'Cruze Regiment, suddenly very embarrassed. There was no doubt in his mind that his Lieutenant had caught him staring at the beautiful new visitor.

'Mastaan, Chhagan... meet Fay, my baby sister. She arrived in Delhi last evening, after a long journey from the snowy hills of Shimla.'

'Nice to meet you, Madam,' said Chhagan, now up on his feet as a show of courtesy to the young lady. His broken diction but correct English made Fay raise her eyebrows in delighted surprise. Not many sepoys of the East India Company spoke the language of their masters.

'Nice to meet you, Ma'am,' said Mastaan. His pronunciation was impeccable. His heart was thumping like a steam engine.

'Oh... my goodness. You speak English... so well!' she exclaimed, a smile beaming across her face as she looked at her brother in evident admiration for his men.

'No, no... don't credit me with Mastaan's English,' clarified the good officer immediately. 'Believe it or not, my dear, as a child he was raised by none other than the great William Fraser himself. That is where our dear friend and the most devastating warrior of the D'Cruze Regiment learnt to speak such good English from.'

'Really? The legendary William Fraser himself??' asked Fay, turning to look directly at Mastaan.

Before Mastaan could respond, Robert D'Cruze continued.

'Yes, Fay. It was William Fraser who taught Mastaan everything – unarmed combat, shooting, swordsmanship, riding, poetry and what not. Why, he even gave Mastaan his name!'

Fay looked straight at Mastaan, stopping her gaze for a moment, as if trying to gauge what kind of a man would emerge, when a supremely gifted native prodigy is groomed by one of the finest British officers that had ever set foot in India. And it was only now that she noticed how strikingly charming Mastaan really was. She had spent several months in India. This had given her the opportunity to dine and dance with not only smart young officers of the Company, but also with several princes and nawabs of this beautiful country.

But not once had she met a man as magnetically attractive as William Fraser's protégé standing in front of her today.

'It is settled then,' declared Robert. 'You both will escort Fay and her friend Patricia to Mehrauli later this month, once she has had the time to unpack and settle-in.'

The infectiously youthful and ever-energetic Fay had expressed her desire to visit the old forts and palaces of the stunning Mughal capital. Her brother, Robert, had decided to hand over the responsibility to his two trusted men.

'But saahab, the road to Mehrauli is not as safe as it used to be. You know that scoundrel Jogi Naagar's tribesmen have been wreaking havoc in those areas these days,' submitted Mastaan politely. His eagerness to spend more time by the side of this golden-haired girl had not overshadowed his sharp soldierly instinct.

'Jogi will not dare attack the Company Bahadur's sepoys, Mastaan. And even if by a remote chance he does commit that blunder, with you and Chhagan around I don't have any reason to worry,' replied Robert.

'The 1st of March then, gentlemen?' asked Fay, looking at Mastaan and Chhagan, her eyes staying a moment longer on the former's face.

'Yes, of course, Madam,' replied Chhagan.

The men saluted their officer and turned to leave. The Subedaar-Major looked at Mastaan with amused eyes as they walked towards their horses. He could sense something was not absolutely normal about his friend's demeanor.

'All okay, Mastaan *baba*?' he asked mischievously.

He was not wrong. The legendary fighter of the D'Cruze Regiment could not get her out of his mind.

The blue-eyed angel.

Fay.

Nikhaal-bhagwaan!

Frontier Tribal Area, Afghanistan Border, February 1857

'Azzaami!'

'Azzzaaaamii!'

'Azzzzaaaaaamii!'

The noise was deafening, as thousands chanted his name in unison - each repetition resounding a hundred-fold louder than the previous one.

The term 'Azzami' in a local dialect of Pashto and in Afghani meant 'one who was fierce as a lion'.

The Pashtun tribesmen of Peshawar were cheering for their local hero – Abu-Zar Pasha.

They could not wait to see their lion claw his way into the white giant's broad chest and tear out his heart. In the seventeen violent years of his undisputed reign across the ravines of western Peshawar, Abu-Zar had beaten the greatest of warriors. The local populace expected nothing different this time.

What they had forgotten was that this time Abu-Zar was not going into combat with just another human.

He was to take on Nikhaal-bhagwaan.

A walking God!

Jon Nicholson was a force of nature.

He feared no one. He seemed to feel no pain. He never fell ill. Even when the most toughened of his men crumbled under trees to rest after a hard night-long march or a long gruesome battle, Nicholson stayed atop his horse under the direct glare of the burning Sun, perched as firmly as a young officer fresh out of his barracks.

It was as if he were a machine – indefatigable, robust, bursting with unnerving cruelty combined with extraordinary valor. And all of this crowned with an insatiable thirst for blood – blood of Britain's enemies. Blood of the East India Company's adversaries.

As he took off his red tunic and loosened his waist-belt and pistol-holster, Nicholson's brawny physique unveiled itself to the spectators of the impending duel. A behemoth by all standards, his muscles rippled like sweating serpents under stretched white hide. His powerful legs pounded the arena like the limbs of a rhinoceros.

And yet, for all his brute ferocity, Nicholson was in front of undoubtedly the most formidable challenger he had ever confronted in his life.

So far.

The opponent to this display of Nicholson's muscle-power was no less daunting himself. As soon as Abu-Zar's arms were released from the ropes that tied them, the Lion of Peshawar rose to his feet, slowly, like a hungry beast readying to pounce on its prey.

The Pasha's eyes appeared to be made of stone, grinding slowly within his eye sockets as he turned to look at Nicholson. They were the confident eyes of a bandit-king accustomed to absolute power and unbridled confidence. The Lion stood as tall as Nicholson himself, and extracted gasps of impressed amazement from his followers when he stretched his arms and shoulders, muscles straining across his torso like iron cables.

The two colossal men looked no different from the monsters written about in the ancient Afghan fables.

'Eeeaaarrgghhh...!!'

It was Nicholson who charged first, screaming like an angry dragon.

The two savage combatants met in the center of the dusty arena like the collision of a pair of battle-elephants. Their fingers interlocked with each other's, as each man tried to twist and break the wrist of the other. When no such result was achieved either way, the Pasha threw his head backwards and rammed it back viciously into the Brigadier General's nose. The effect was immediate. While Abu-Zar himself staggered and reeled in pain, Nicholson's nose and mouth spat blood almost instantly.

A roar went up from the Pashtun herdsmen as they relished seeing the blow from their local hero and the ongoing combat. For them, the crimson drops of Nicholson's blood on the sands of Peshawar were the sweetest payback to the foreign invaders who had stolen their lands and defiled the ethos of their ancestors.

But the celebration was premature. Nicholson used his palm to wipe the dripping blood from his nose and rubbed the red liquid all over his own face and chest – a grotesque act that gave him the appearance of a ghoul. He then growled in the manner of a fiend and charged at the Pasha, landing a powerful fist into the Afghan's ribs. The bandit coughed in suffering but retaliated like the seasoned fighter that he was.

The battle had begun.

For the next several minutes every imaginable method of inflicting pain was deployed by the two bloodthirsty warriors. One was fighting for his freedom and his name. The other was battling to establish the rule of his Company and his Queen.

Punching, clawing, biting, strangling each other... the two men ensured that the sand of the arena was sprinkled with generous showers of British and Afghan blood.

The Company's sepoys were under strict instructions by their Brigadier General. Even if this duel resulted in the Englishman's death at the hands of the bandit-king, no soldier of the East India Company had the permission to intervene.

Despite being surrounded by over three thousand armed men who worshipped him, Nicholson had made it clear.

This was indeed a fight unto death.

Minutes passed like years.

Both men were now on their knees, drenched in sweat and blood, gasping for breath. Like two wounded tigers drawing on their last reservoir of strength and spirit, they tried to get back on their feet – for another, and probably the last, round of combat.

It was the Lion who succeeded first in bringing his massive body to balance on his feet. He began to stumble across the muddy ring towards Nicholson. But very soon he broke into a run, smashing his knee brutally into the Britisher's throat.

'Hooaaaarrrgghh...!' groaned Nicholson in what was evidently indescribable pain, before crashing to the ground like a log of timber.

'Azzaami...'

'Azzzaaammmi...' mumbled Abu-Zar from his bloodied mouth, spreading his arms and gesturing to the thousands of Pashtuns in audience to resume chanting his name.

His countrymen did not disappoint him.

'Azzaami!'

'Azzzaaaamii!'

'Azzzzaaaaaamii!'

The entire province now exploded with the roar of the people of Peshawar.

The Lion now moved towards his enemy to deliver the winning blow. Nicholson lay in a pool of his own blood, writhing in pain.

Abu-Zar stepped over the Englishman's collapsed frame and grabbed the fallen man's head in his own gigantic hands. Like a man possessed with inhuman hate, he kept beating his head in rhythm with the chanting of his own name.

'Azzaami!'

'Azzzaaaamii!'

He gripped the bearded chin of Nicholson in one hand and then spread his other monstrous hand across the Brigadier General's head.

He looked up at the sepoys surrounding the ring, mocking them in ruthless cruelty. The soldiers of the East India Company were veteran enough to know what Abu-Zar was going to do next. His grip was a giveaway. He was going to break Jon Nicholson's neck.

'Bad move coming so close, Pasha...' a voice whispered in broken Pashto.

To the utter bewilderment of the Lion, the words came from somewhere very close. They came from right under him.

The snake-like eyes of Nicholson were now staring deep into the Pasha's soul. The bandit knew instinctively that it was the last thing he would ever see.

Like a bunch of blunt spears emerging from below the sandy earth, the thick fingers of Nicholson's right hand pierced into Abu-Zar's throat, tearing the so-called Lion's jugular into shreds. As Pasha twisted and sputtered in pain holding on to Nicholson's wrist, the gigantic Englishman rose to his feet.

In a morbid display of his notorious savagery, the dreaded Brigadier General now shoved four fingers deep into the struggling bandit's throat, twisted them and began to summarily tear open the vanquished fighter's neck holding his jaw. Soon the Lion's head appeared to be connected with nothing but foot-long stretched chords of vein and muscle to the rest of his thrashing body. To the utter disgust and shudder of even his own men, who were not strangers to his unspeakable brutality, Jon Nicholson ripped out the head of Abu-Zar Pasha with his bare hands.

'*THIS* IS YOUR LION?' he screamed, dangling the Pasha's head, clutching the dead man's long hair.

The white killer turned around to the thousands that were now hushed into shocked silence.

'*THIS* IS YOUR LION...?' he yelled again, his neck veins ready to explode.

Holding the decapitated head of Abu-Zar Pasha, unmoved by the blood pouring out from the bandit-king's lifeless skull... Jon Nicholson stamped his ruthless superiority deep into the hearts and minds of the native populace.

Yet again.

It was now the turn of the Brigadier General's sepoys to raise their fearsome chant. They erupted all at once, their fists in the air and their muskets firing shots by the hundreds.

'*'Nikhaal-bhagwaan ki... JAI!'*'

Victory to the God Nikhaal!

A Midnight Meeting

Tughlaqabad, Outskirts of Delhi, February 1857

'We are under oath to protect the Company Bahadur!' said Mastaan, nearly shouting within a whisper.

As they approached the secret rendezvous, Chhagan raised his finger to his lips, indicating to his friend to not utter even a word more.

The fort of Tughlaqabad now lay in ruins. Built in the year 1321 by the Delhi Sultanate ruler Ghiyas-ud-din Tughlaq as an impregnable stronghold against the marauding Mongol hordes, it was abandoned in the year 1327. Cursed by the Sufi saint Hazrat Nizamuddin Auliya, the fort was destined for decay and devastation.

It was in the middle of the night and chilly winds whistled across miles of barren lands surrounding the deserted medieval castle. As they made their way up through the stony rabble of the fort's entrance, Mastaan protested again.

'This is all a big mistake, Chhagnu. Who are we going to meet at this unearthly hour? How do you know the Company

Bahadur is not in the know of this clandestine meeting? Worse still, how do you know we are not walking into a trap laid out by the Company itself?!'

Chhagan did not respond. He seemed to be in a trance. The Subedaar-Major kept climbing up across the outer walls of the fort and into an arched dome far inside. From a distance Mastaan could see a lit fire. Around the crackling flames, on the tall and curved walls of the dome, loomed the ominous shadows of some mysterious men.

It was a gathering of eight.

Two each from the East India Company's nearest cantonments surrounding Delhi.

In attendance was the Subedaar-Major of the Meerut chhaavani, the man who had written the secret letter to Chhagan. He was accompanied by an aging cavalryman, clearly a battle-hardened veteran and an unofficial leader of the Meerut Regiments' sepoys.

Two other men, dressed in dirty white tunics betraying the long journey they had endured on horseback, represented the soldiers of the Cawnpore (Kanpur) cantonment.

And finally, there was the fierce-looking commander, with his menacing man-at-arms by his side clutching a gleaming, unsheathed sword. Seated on a stone platform directly in the glow of the yellow-red fire, this authoritative man was tall and bulky. He sported thick sideburns with an enormous handlebar moustache and exuded a domineering persona.

He was none other than the widely revered Subedaar of the massive Bareilly Brigade, the Rohilla Pashtun and veteran of the First Anglo-Afghan War – Bakht Khan.

'*Pranaam*,' Chhagan wished the seated commander politely as they walked up to the waiting party.

'*Khush rahiye*,' replied Bakht Khan in a booming voice. 'Be well.'

The commander from Bareilly then shifted his gaze to the long-haired warrior accompanying Chhagan Dubey, expecting another respectful salutation.

None came.

'This is Mastaan, Khan saahab,' said Chhagan, trying to diffuse the mild tension he sensed between the two men instantly.

'Oh... Mastaaaaan?!' replied Bakht Khan with a broad grin, wide eyes and unhidden admiration. 'So, this is the famous Mastaan... the fabulous *Bandookbaaz* of the D'Cruze Regiment?'

Mastaan couldn't care less for the awe-struck reaction of the Bareilly commander. Heroes' tales travel far. And the feared Subedaar of the D'Cruze Regiment was used to such wonderment as people met him.

Ignoring the praise that Bakht Khan went on to shower upon him, Mastaan couldn't help but strain his ears.

Tumma Tumma... Tumm!

Tumma Tumma... Tumm!

He felt he could hear the faint sound of a beating drum somewhere far. He brushed away the thought. They were in the middle of cold wilderness, surrounded on all sides by rocky arid wasteland, wild animals and bandits.

No one can be around this haunted citadel at this ghostly hour.

'No soldier born of a Hindu mother's womb will bite into those cartridges, Chhagan!' roared Bakht Khan.

'Nor would a true follower of Islam!' added one of the soldiers from Cawnpore. He sported a bold saffron-red *teeka* on his forehead.

'The firangis have invited their own destruction with such a degenerate scheme to corrupt our religion, Khan saahab,' said Hariya Thakur, the veteran fighter from Meerut, seething with rage.

It was now Chhagan's turn to speak.

'We must all rise together, brothers. All chhaavanis, all brigades, all regiments, every single gun... all at once! If called upon to do so, I, Chhagan Dubey, will consider it an honor to be the one to fire the first shot of the revolution. And mark my words... this will not be just a mutiny or a rebellion by any measure. This will be a war for the independence of our motherland!'

'And how is that, Chhagan?' snapped Mastaan out of nowhere.

'How is this anything but a dishonorable revolt? Why will this not be a mutiny when we are pledged to serve...'

Tumma Tumma... Tumm!

Tumma Tumma... Tumm!

It was now unmissable. There was indeed someone playing a percussion instrument of some sort, in a hideous rhythm. And the ill-omened beat was inching closer.

Trained troopers as they were, all eight men drew their swords in anticipation of imminent danger. As they turned towards the dilapidated pillar from behind which the beating sound now seemed to emanate, they were startled at what sneakily emerged from the shadows.

A half-naked *fakeer* with broken teeth, deranged eyes and the mad laughter of someone who has a vision into a ghastly future, crept out into the open.

Tumma Tumma... Tumm!

Tumma Tumma... Tumm!

He mocked the eight men, fearlessly beating his half-torn lambskin *dhapli* – hobbling, laughing, howling and crying all at once...

...unmistakably like the cold harbinger of death.

An Immortal Brahmin

Barrackpore, Bengal Provinces, February 1857

'Oh, come on, *pundit ji*,' remarked the shy brahmin soldier.

He somehow managed to hide the storm brewing in his heart under a beaming, youthful smile... and some generous swigs of *bhaang thandai* (a cold, condensed milk drink spiked with marijuana).

Something told him that let alone immortality, even his remaining few days were starkly numbered.

'*Arey*, I am serious... you have immortality written all over the lines of your palm, my son!' the pundit insisted. 'You will live forever!'

Delighted as always with the make-believe outcome of his weekly tryst with the local palmist, the strapping 29-year-old sepoy dropped a few coins into the priest's sandalwood bowl. However, despite all his attempts to please the Gods in heaven through ritual baths at dawn and incessant chanting of the holy mantras, he couldn't help but rebuke himself... over and over again.

A Hindu forced to savor the fat of a cow is worse than dead.

'I will take leave of you now, pundit ji,' said the dusky, handsome sepoy.

'Be well, my son. Just remember... *Bharatvarsha* or Hindustan will always remember your name. You are timeless... eternal!'

The priest was not lying. He was also not trying to fool the young, intoxicated and guilt-stricken sepoy. He was fully convinced. The planets had spoken loud and clear through the lines on the rifle-roughened palms of this soldier.

Mangal Pandey *was* destined for immortality.

He was a soldier in the 34th Bengal Native Infantry.

As he poured a few drops of milk over the ancient *Shiva-linga* that lay placed under a massive tree on the way back to his barracks, Mangal noticed a stout man at a distance. Wrapped in a shawl, the man stood with his hands folded in obeisance to Shiva. But he dared not come close to the revered idol.

In a jiffy Mangal knew what was holding the man back from touching his beloved deity. He witnessed such men every day, much to his consternation.

This is not the Sanatana dharma I was taught.

'Come closer, my friend!' he called out to the man in the shawl, gesticulating and inviting him to step closer to Shiva.

The man in the distance hesitated for a second. In the very next moment, he turned hastily to leave. But Mangal was in no mood to relent. Not today. Not anymore. Enough had been done to destroy his dharma, his religion, his people's way-of-life and his motherland. Enough fault-lines had been created by those in power.

He ran after the man and grabbed him by the arm.

'Let me go!' mumbled the man from behind the shawl covering his face and mouth, struggling to free his arm from Mangal Pandey's strong grip.

'But why, brother? Stay and pray as long as you want. Come with me. I will take you to the Shiva-linga and stand guard to make sure no one dares object. He belongs as much to you as he does to me.'

The man stopped struggling. From the narrow opening in the rough cloth that wrapped him he stared into Mangal's eyes. He then spoke in a voice that Pandey could swear he recognized.

'Shiva is *not* as much mine as He is yours, Mangal,' the man continued.

With these words he took off the woolen veil from his face.

It was *Jamadaar* Quartermaster Ishwari Prasad, Mangal Pandey's superior in the 5th Company of the 34th Bengal Native Infantry.

And yet, somehow, he was not Mangal's superior in life.

The East India Company had further fanned the divide between the so-called upper castes and lower castes. Between Hindus and Muslims. Between the rich and the poor. Between the landlord and the peasant. Between Indian and Indian.

Within the walls of the cantonment, Ishwari Prasad was a non-commissioned officer of the British East India Company.

Outside its walls, however, he was a low-caste native.

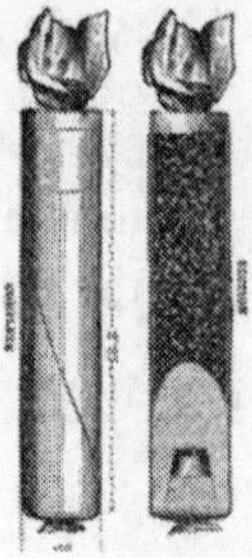

Mutiny

Tughlaqabad, Outskirts of Delhi, February 1857

The lunatic laughed again, rolling and bruising his ugly, emaciated body on the sharp stones of the cursed ruins.

His horrendous lambskin instrument did not rest even for a moment.

Tumma Tumma... Tumm!

Tumma Tumma... Tumm!

'A party of dead men! A party of dead men! Another party of dead men!' the madman yelled in glee.

He twirled like a scrawny goblin, stopping and staring at the blank indigo skies every few moments... before breaking into his mad dance again.

Before the eight warriors in front of him could figure out how to react to this insane display of inexplicable horror, the twisted fakeer suddenly dropped his voice and whispered to them, as if sharing a dark secret.

'Do you know who the others were who came to this fort to conspire against a common enemy? Tell me... tell me... do you know... do you know?'

Much as his fearsome lunacy and grotesque behavior had struck fear in their hearts, the men feigned nonchalance.

Bakht Khan turned to the others.

'This is a crazy man. Let us get back to our discussion. There is very little time.'

'Very little time! Very little time! Very little time... for the walking dead!' the maniac repeated after Bakht Khan.

He was trying to tell them something.

It was decided.

After two hours of rigorous conference, battle-planning and studying of rough maps of the roads, British garrisons and *topkhaanas* (artillery) around Delhi, the date for the so-called Mutiny was zeroed down on.

'1st of June it is then, Khan saahab,' announced Chhagan, as he looked up from a rolled open calendar. Melodramatic as he always liked to be, the Subedaar-Major drew out his dagger and stabbed it into the square that marked the date he had just declared.

'You are right, Chhagan,' responded Bakht Khan. 'The 1st of June it is! I will inform the forces of Nana Saaheb and Tantya Tope as well.'

Mastaan could not hold himself back any longer.

'You know what I think? I think all of you have sold your blackened souls! The East India Company is our employer. We have consumed its salt for years. Today, we gather here as warriors and trained military-men with great pride and arrogance. But have you thought about it - *who* has made us the men we are today? The Company Bahadur! Who has imparted combat-skills to us? The Company Bahadur! Today the homes and hearths of tens of thousands of sipahis run on the wages paid by the Company. Today when we ride into any town, city or village across all of Hindustan, people bow and clear the path for us. Our bellies are full. Our guns are loaded. Our uniforms sparkle and our barracks are superior to the huts any of us have back home. And *this* is the Company you all want to revolt against? Why? Just because some debauched kings of some exploited and poverty-stricken provinces were dethroned? Those kings and nawabs were rolling in ill-acquired luxury and riches when their populace was dying *en masse*. You want to mutiny against the East India Company for *that*?'

Chhagan got up from his crouched position over the map and took a few steps towards Mastaan. His face was twitching with anger.

'Look here, Mastaan... I have had enough of your preaching about...'

Before he could complete his sentence, Dubey felt a hand on his shoulder. It was Bakht Khan. The commander nodded slightly at the Subedaar-Major, indicating that now he wanted to take the debate with the hero of D'Cruze Regiment forward.

Bakht Khan moved closer to Mastaan, locked his eyes with the legendary fighter of Delhi and spoke with an air of superiority... in both rank seniority as well as in wisdom.

'Why do you keep using the word *mutiny*, Mastaan? Or, for that matter, the term *revolt*?' he asked, his hands folded across his chest and his tone disturbingly self-assured.

Mastaan rolled up his eyes for a split moment. He found the question preposterous. Patience was anyway not one of his virtues.

'What else is this if not a mutiny, Khan saahab?' he replied in a dismissive tone.

The commander from Bareilly stood his ground undaunted. He laughed and asked the next question.

'Would it still be called a mutiny, Mastaan, if it is fought against those who are the most unscrupulous mutineers themselves?'

'Everything we hold dear...'

Barrackpore, Bengal, February 1857

As Ishwari poured milk and tears on to the holy linga of Shiva, his hands trembled with boundless joy.

It was not every day that an outcaste was seen worshipping the Lord so closely, touching and propitiating Shiva with his own hands. As a result, a crowd began to gather around the temple under the tree shade.

'This is sacrilege!' a voice boomed from amid the steadily growing mob that now surrounded the open-air shrine.

'The holy temple is defiled!' screamed the shrill voice of a woman.

Jamadaar Ishwari hesitated for a moment and stopped his worship midway. The burgeoning mob around the temple was making him very anxious. His eyes turned to Mangal, who nodded gently and slowly shut his eyelids, urging Ishwari to continue.

'We will not let this blasphemy continue,' shouted a young man with a sword-like moustache. He brandished a shining and well-oiled *lathi* (cane staff). 'Step forward, my fellow men! Let us teach these outcastes a lesson!'

His bravado did not last long.

Mangal Pandey caught hold of one end of his flowing white robe and flung it around his neck like a muffler of sorts. This one action was enough to reveal the gleaming scimitar that hung from the sepoy's waist.

The next few minutes passed in hushed silence, as the Jamadaar of the East India Company showered his love on his deity fearlessly.

As the duo of Mangal and Ishwari was leaving the shrine of Shiva, faceless voices erupted from the crowd once again.

'Shame!'

'Shame on a brahmin to sully a temple like this!'

Pandey did not flinch. He held on to Ishwari Prasad's arm and kept walking.

'Shame on you, sipahi Pandey, for forgetting your high caste and your duty!'

'It is false brahmins like you who are causing our dharma to lose its sheen!'

Now this was going too far. Mangal Pandey stopped in his stride, turned around and stared at the gathering in the manner of a raging bull.

'High caste, did one of you say? Dharma... is that what you are worried about?' he challenged the men and women surrounding them.

As his glare moved from face to face, he identified some he knew and loved.

'Manohar *chacha*... you are most learned. You tell me... when Lord Vishnu took the avatar of Shri Krishna, was he born as a brahmin? Or did he choose the household of a cowherd, a *yadava*?'

The crowd was silent.

'You tell me, Imarti *taayi*... you have read the scriptures. When Shiva took the form of a *kiraat* and fought the great warrior Arjuna, was he a kshatriya? Or a simple dweller from a jungle tribe? Why, he even descended to our world as a simple *machhuara* or fisherman when he wanted to woo *Maa* Parvati back to Kailasa.'

The large group of people was now completely mute. One, they did not have answers to Mangal Pandey's observations. And two, none of them had expected a simple sepoy of the Company to present such profound arguments.

Mangal Pandey was a man way ahead of his time.

'Remember, Manohar chacha... remember, Imarti taayi... remember all of you, my brothers and sisters... our Maker has made us all equal. This Ishwari here is a child of the same God as you and I are. Until when will we keep fighting among ourselves, and let white men from beyond the great seas come and rule over our collective destinies? Until when will we tear open our own villages, towns and society in the name of religion and caste, while the Company Bahadur takes away everything we hold dear?!'

By the end of his monologue, Mangal Pandey was speaking at the highest pitch of his voice. His eyes were on fire, questioning every soul that stood across them.

Waiting for a moment or two to calm his heavy breathing, he turned to leave, still holding on to Ishwari Prasad.

'They will take away everything we hold dear... everything... we... hold... dear,' he whispered as he left, unsure whether he was speaking to the gathered audience or to himself.

The Eternal Spell of Mahbub-e-Ilahi

Tughlaqabad, Outskirts of Delhi, February 1857

'And what, may I ask, is a mutiny, Mastaan?' insisted Bakht Khan.

The commander from Bareilly spoke with the moral authority of someone who knows a lot more than his debating counterpart, and someone who has great conviction in his cause.

'I do not know what you are trying to say, Khan saahab...' replied Mastaan.

Bakht Khan smiled.

'We are only trying to restore the rightful order, Mastaan. Do you know *who* the real mutineers are... in every single sense of the word?'

The honesty in Khan's voice was now beginning to catch the attention of D'Cruze Regiment's supreme fighter.

'Please stop talking in puzzles and say what you have to say, Khan saa'b,' Mastaan asked in a tone slightly politer than before.

'It is the East India Company that is the real traitor, Mastaan. I am surprised someone as famously knowledgeable as you are missing the entire point here. Allow me to explain. In 1612, when the Company first landed on the ports of Surat and Calcutta as a diplomatic visitation under Sir Thomas Roe, it was the Mughal Emperor Jehangir who ruled over almost entire Hindustan and beyond from his capital in Agra. It was with the Mughal monarch's blessings and under his absolute and unquestioned sovereignty that the Company accepted to carry on its trade. For several decades the Company continued to pay taxes and homage to the Mughal court and minted coins under the over-lordship of the Mughal Badshah. Every time the Company Bahadur tried to flex its muscles, it was cut to size – like in 1689 when Aurangzeb's general, Siddi Yaqub, attacked Bombay and the East India Company faced a humiliating defeat, forcing its officers to beg Emperor Aurangzeb for mercy.'

Mastaan was listening intently. So were Chhagan and the others. What Bakht Khan was elucidating had the potential to change belief-systems and alter the inner-voices of Company loyalists.

The commander from Bareilly now walked back to his stony seat, lit a *chillum* of tobacco with a red coal and continued the discourse.

'For over one hundred years, the East India Company operated as nothing more than a trading company permitted to conduct its business under the license of the Mughal sultanate. For decades, till as recently as a few years ago, the Company circulated its coins and currency under the dominion of the Mughal Emperor. All of the Company's business was conducted in the name of the Mughal king, and, for all practical and theoretical purposes – it was the East India Company that was the servant of the monarch of Delhi and not the other way around!'

Bakht Khan took a long drag from his chillum and let the blue smoke out into the darkness of the night sky.

He then turned to Mastaan, who appeared to be in a mild daze from the revelations just made. Mastaan knew some of these facts, but not all. Certainly not enough to appreciate how it was actually the Mughal throne that was at the receiving end of the mutiny of the East India Company. From what Bakht Khan had just explained, it was beyond doubt the Company Bahadur that was the real rebel – changing its color from a docile merchant outfit bending its knee at the Mughal court, to a ruthlessly opportunistic land-devouring dragon.

Mastaan had understood what the Bareilly commander was trying to say. Bakht Khan completed his account nonetheless.

'In reality, when they humiliated and subverted Bahadur Shah Zafar and his predecessors, when they wrested control of large swathes of territory from the Mughal dynasty, when they marched in massive armies into the cantonments of Delhi, when they all but imprisoned the Mughal king in his own palace - it was the Company Bahadur that was brazenly mutinying against its native masters.

So, you see, Mastaan... you are trying to side with the tormentor.

Not with the victim.'

They were now walking back to their waiting horses. In complete silence.

As they reached their mounts, Mastaan rested his head on his horse's saddle and gave out a big sigh.

'What happened, brother?' asked Chhagan. 'Too much to take in for a day, isn't it?'

Mastaan nodded silently.

He then turned to his friend, looking completely exasperated.

'What now, Chhagnu? What are we headed towards??'

Chhagan let go of his horse's reign and turned to his friend incredulously.

'There is going to be a sepoy revolt of gigantic proportions, Mastaan!' he exclaimed, his eyes now wide with excitement and hate. 'A great war for the independence of our *maatribhoomi*, our homeland... my brother!'

'And where will it all end, Chhagnu? Do you foresee the ocean of blood this is going to unleash? Can you not foretell the catastrophe we are galloping towards?'

Chhagan walked a few steps and came face to face with his dearest friend. He kept his hands on Mastaan's shoulders and spoke in a reassuring tone.

'It will all unfold as we have planned, Mastaan baba. We have the numbers. We have the guns. It will be a breeze. From Barrackpore in Bengal to the Laal Qila in Delhi, our men will take back all that is ours. This is the end of British hegemony, Mastaan.'

Mastaan smiled weakly, but the joy did not reach his terrified eyes. He could not believe the naivety of his beloved friend.

What Chhagan Dubey and many others like him forgot was that violence not only proliferates violence, it also spawns exponentially more vicious counter-violence.

'You are being silly, Mastaan. Nothing will happen to fine officers like D'Cruze saahab or their families,' replied Chhagan confidently, as they trudged their way out of the Tughlaqabad Fort exteriors. 'This is a war for our freedom from the East India Company's injustice, their greed and their mindless violence. We are never going to become like them. Our countrymen are not as heartless as the firangis, my friend. We will fight the war with honor.'

Chhagan Dubey was not well-informed. He did not know that every war in history that turned into a heinous bloodlust was started by a few seemingly righteous men, under the name of honor, of nation, of religion and of justice.

Human beings never failed to let their own kind down, over and over again.

'If I knew what the agenda of this meeting was, I would have advised against this cursed venue, Chhagnu,' said Mastaan.

'What do you mean?'

'Do you know what that mad fakeer was trying to tell us?' asked Mastaan, turning to look at Chhagan Dubey, who was now riding next to him. 'Why was he referring to us as a party of dead men? Do you know who were the unfortunate men that once gathered on a similar dark night, in this very fort, to plan their offensive against a common enemy?'

The Subedaar-Major was clueless.

'Who are you talking about?' he asked cautiously.

'It was the mid-18th century noblemen of the Delhi regime, Chhagnu. The men who fought against the cold-blooded marauder, Nadir Shah, in March 1739 at the Battle of Karnal. They swore to combine their forces under these very haunted domes, and together hailed what they believed was going to be the end of the Persian invader. You do know where they all went, right?'

'Oh, come on, Mastaan... you are being ridiculous now! Since when have *you* started believing in these silly folklores?'

'I don't believe in folklores or hollow legends, Chhagnu. But I do believe in the eternal spell of Hazrat Nizamuddin Auliya, the *Mahbub-e-Ilahi* or Beloved of God.'

It was only now that a chilling realization hit the Subedaar-Major of the D'Cruze Regiment like a bolt of lightning.

The fort of Tughlaqabad was still under the eternal, haunting curse of Saint Nizamuddin Auliya.

Hunuz Dilli door ast, the revered Sufi had said.

Delhi is still far away.

True to the words of the immortal saint, those who sought refuge in and breathed the air of the ill-omened fortress of Tughlaqabad – were *never* to rule Delhi for long.

'He will avenge me!'

Barrackpore, Bengal, 1st March 1857

The red tunic now seemed to weigh a thousand tons.

His hands trembled as he buttoned up his uniform.

The word on the streets could not be wrong. Every roadside huddle, every gathering around sweetmeat shops, every group at opium dens, every cluster of women at the bathing ghaats... all were speaking about only one potent rumor.

The beef-and-pork-greased cartridges from Calcutta.

As his forehead dripped with sweat, the faces of his ancestors danced in front of his bloodshot eyes. Mangal's entire body began to shiver. With every brass-button that he hooked into place, he felt as if he was betraying his blood, his forefathers and the *mitti* he was born from.

At this time of debilitating angst and a crushing sense of guilt, it was Ishwari Prasad who came to Mangal's rescue. The dawn bugle had been sounded and sepoys of the 34th Bengal Native Infantry were gearing up for the morning parade.

'What is the matter, brother? Are you alright?' asked Prasad, worried at his friend's overly anxious appearance this morning.

Mangal seemed to emerge from a spell.

'Huh... yes... yes, I am fine,' he replied.

He fixed his tunic and tightened his belts and buckles. He picked up his Brown Bess Musket, that was soon to be replaced by the new Enfield P-53 rifles from Ambala.

As the two men made their way out of the sepoy barracks and on to the parade ground, Mangal Pandey was stopped and held back by a hand on his shoulder. Ishwari Prasad wanted to have a word.

'What is the matter, Mangal?' asked the Quartermaster once again.

This time he got an answer.

'I will *never* bite into those blasphemous cartridges, Ishwari bhai...'

The determination on Mangal's face was cast in iron.

Ishwari Prasad turned to look at sepoy Pandey and spoke in a hushed voice.

'Look, Mangal... we are all under deep duress at the prospect of sullying our faith irreversibly by putting cow and pig fat into our mouths. But the news is not confirmed, my brother. Some men approached the Commanding Officer General

Hearsey, who firmly denied any such action by the British. Hearsey reassured us against any attempt by the Company Bahadur to convert all of us to *Issai* dharma.'

'That is all a big lie, Ishwari bhai!' retorted Mangal. 'Have you not heard what our brothers from the 19th Bengal Native Infantry did two days ago at Behrampore? They refused to bite into these cartridges, even at the cost of being declared and penalized as mutineers. Why do you think they refused in the first place? There is no doubt now! The firangis want to destroy our belief, our dharma from its very roots. They have already inflicted enough damage – pitching brother against brother in the name of caste and religion. I will not let them harm us further, Ishwari bhai. What will remain of us if we are stripped off even the last remnants of our culture, our philosophies and our glorious past? Either we accept being turned into infidels by tasting the flesh of *gau-maata*, or we take up arms against such a ruthless oppressor!'

'Shhhhh... do not be a fool, Mangal!' cautioned the Quartermaster, his voice strained, as he pushed Mangal Pandey against a wall. 'Not even a word about this! Much as everyone is flexing muscles in the privacy of barrack dormitories and making tall promises at the bhaang dens, no one will stand by your side. Not *one* of these soldiers will aim his gun at a European!'

Sepoy Pandey grinned. His eyes were moist, but his face radiated a strange kind of joy.

'I know they won't. Not on the first day. But when I am gone, my soul will ignite all of Hindustan to rise and rid itself of these cruel firangis. Wait and see, Ishwari bhai, our countrymen will unite.

We will become independent of the British, even if it takes a whole century from now... give or take ten years.'

As the two of them stepped out on to the sunny parade ground to participate in the Brigade's morning drill, Mangal Pandey shared a personal detail with Ishwari Prasad.

A detail that he was most proud of.

'I assure you, Ishwari bhai... I am not as alone as I appear to be. There is one man who will rise and strike terror into the hearts of the firangis once he hears that Mangal Pandey has fallen. And believe me, that one fighter is equal to a hundred of the Company's elite combat troops.

He will avenge me!'

With these words, Mangal Pandey strode down the ground, parading as smartly as any British sepoy or officer.

What Ishwari Prasad did not know was that Mangal's father, Divakar Pandey, had an older brother, whose name was late sipahi Ram Narayan Pandey.

What Ishwari Prasad did not know was that Mangal had a beloved first cousin, a formidable older brother... far away in Delhi.

His name was Mastaan.

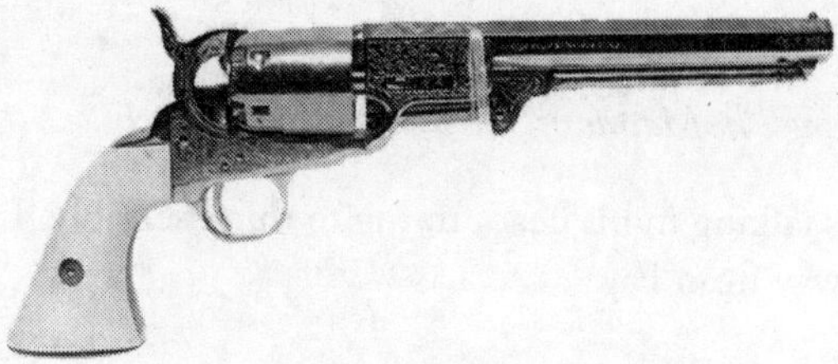

Bandookbaaz!

Mehrauli, Outskirts of Delhi, 1st March 1857

Mastaan's beautiful long locks fluttered in the cool breeze, as he led the procession into the forests surrounding the Mughal Emperor's summer palace in Mehrauli.

Fay's horse was right behind Mastaan's, and it was not so by accident. For a large part of their tour, the beautiful English girl was staring more at the smashing Subedaar of the D'Cruze Regiment than at the monuments and palaces that they had toured around.

What she did not know, and Mastaan did not allow his actions or expressions to betray, was that the splendid warrior was equally smitten by her, supremely conscious of her presence every moment of their journey. His fingertips were still fragrant with the lavender perfume from Fay's delicate wrist, as he had helped her mount her horse at Lieutenant D'Cruze's residence a couple of hours ago. Every word she spoke rang like the jingle of a *ghungroo* in his head. Every time she laughed, he felt that the gardens and the flowers laughed with her.

She is English, Mastaan. She is beyond your reach.

He was talking in his head, trying to think sensibly. Trying to keep away from Fay.

In futility.

They were a party of sixteen – Fay, her cheerful, shy friend Patricia, Subedaar-Major Chhagan Dubey, sepoy Balram Rai, sepoy Shahbaaz, ten sawaars of the D'Cruze Regiment and Subedaar Mastaan.

Being the most educated and most fluent in English among his Hindustani compatriots, the onus of playing the role of a tour guide fell on Mastaan's shoulders.

'You have already seen the Emperor's summer palace and the towering Qutub Minar, my lady. What we see ahead of us is the tomb of the Delhi Sultanate ruler Ghiyasuddin Balban. This was built in the 13th century...'

'Why were you named Mastaan?'

There was silence for a few moments as Fay's youthful voice rang out from ten feet behind the tour guide.

An embarrassed Mastaan turned momentarily to look at Fay, before turning his gaze back on the road. He could sense Chhagnu, Balram, Shahbaaz and even Pat smiling mischievously.

But the lovely Fay was unfazed. She had ignored the details of Sultan Balban's tomb and had interrupted Mastaan, making no secret of her obvious fondness for him. She had held herself back for several weeks. She had spent every single day lost in the thoughts of the ruggedly handsome man she had met at her brother's garden-meeting. But this morning, seeing him just a grasp away, Fay could not bear the distance anymore.

'I am asking you something, Mastaan. I hear William Fraser gave you this unusual name. Tell me about it.'

With this Fay spurred her horse on and joined Mastaan at the front of their small procession. She could not stay away any longer. She could not go on quietly resisting the intense magnetism of this extraordinary man.

The Subedaar of the D'Cruze Regiment turned to look at her. In an instant he caught her glance and looked straight into her deep blue eyes. In that one look he wanted her to comprehend everything – how much she had begun to mean to him despite just two meetings, how helpless he felt in this situation, how bewitchingly beautiful he found her to be and how impossible their union of any kind was.

He wanted Fay to understand everything in that one look.

And she did.

'As a boy, during our sword-fight training sessions, I was unbeaten for years. Even veteran sawaars of the Company Bahadur found it hard to stay in the ring with me,' began Mastaan, sounding as humble as could.

'Not just one sawaar at a time, Madam. Even half a dozen skilled swordsmen together could not outperform our magic-lad here,' added Chhagan merrily. He could sense how impressed the young girl was with his friend.

'Is that so...?' Fay asked, turning to Mastaan, once again raising her eyebrows in that typically adorable way.

Mastaan's heart skipped a beat as their eyes met once again. This time it was Fay who was trying to say something. Her eyes wanted Mastaan to see many things – that she was falling for him hopelessly, that she did not care for the differences in their lives and their backgrounds, and that she was willing to fight for him if he was willing to fight for her.

Seeing that his friend was evidently tongue-tied and lost in the eyes of this young English girl, Chhagan decided to intervene yet again.

'It was for his unmatched prowess with the scimitar that Fraser saahab named him after a great Persian sword, Madam – the undefeated *shamsheer – Mastaan*!'

Fay did not react. She was delighted to know every little incremental detail about this magnificent man. But she wanted to hear everything from him directly. She wanted to be alone with him.

She continued to stare at Mastaan unabashedly, unconcerned with their surroundings.

Their mesmeric gaze was interrupted by another voice. This time is was sawaar Shahbaaz, speaking in broken yet easily comprehensible English.

'There is another name that he is known by, Madam. It is a name given to him by the brave men of his paltan,' said Shahbaaz loudly yet respectfully, as he rode next to Pat's horse.

'Really? And what is that name now?' enquired Pat. Fay and Mastaan's electric attraction was now palpable. Patricia saw that her friend was getting desperately weak in the knees.

'*Bandookbaaz!*' shouted Chhagan, Shahbaaz, Balram and the ten sawaars in practiced unison.

Both Fay and Pat broke into a laugh at the jolly melodrama of these fine native men. An embarrassed Mastaan hid his face momentarily in his own palm.

'What does... *bandutbaa*... mean?' asked Fay, unable to pronounce the word in the first go.

Chhagan Dubey now smiled politely and spoke in a tone filled with love, admiration and respect for his marvelous friend.

'The entire East India Company and all the armies of the Nawabs of Hindustan know Mastaan by the title of Bandookbaaz, Madam. It loosely means – the Gunman.

Our Mastaan is not just a master swordsman, Fay Madam. He is also Hindustan's fastest and finest marksman.'

Fay nodded and smiled admiringly at Mastaan, who was now self-conscious beyond words and continued to look straight ahead.

She leaned forward on her horse and strained her neck to be able to look into his eyes playfully. When he looked back, she mouthed a word softly – only for him to see.

'Bandookbaaz.'

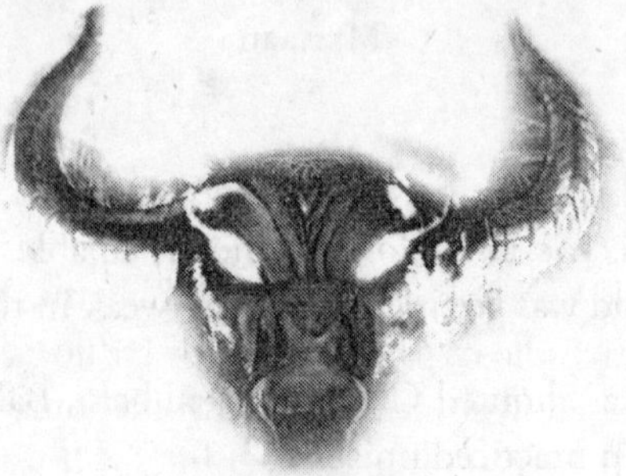

Jogi

Mehrauli, Outskirts of Delhi, 1st March 1857

It was getting dark, much to both Mastaan and Chhagan's worry.

The outing they had planned in and around Mehrauli was supposed to last only a few hours, and they were to be back within the safety of the cantonment before sundown. But the playful enthusiasm and lazy picnic mood of the two English girls touring with them had upset their schedule. They were minutes away from sunset and still deep in the heart of the forests of Mehrauli.

This was bandit territory. It was ruled by a tribal warlord, whom Mastaan and Chhagan had vanquished in the past. But he was still one of the most dangerous men in northern Hindustan.

And he was hungry for revenge.

'Should we send out a rider to the chhaavani and bring in reinforcements, Mastaan?' asked Chhagan. 'It will take a couple of hours. We can wait here and avoid riding through the thickest end of the jungle with just ten or twelve men.'

Mastaan thought for a moment and replied.

'No, I think we should press on, Chhagnu. Waiting for a sawaar to reach the cantt and then for reinforcements to ride back all the way will mean at least four hours. By now Jogi knows we are here, and he is watching us. If we wait, we will be stranded in his territory with these ladies for too long in the dark, needlessly provoking him. Let's get out of the forest as soon as we can.'

Mastaan had barely completed his sentence when a menacing-looking man appeared in front of them, riding leisurely on a huge horse painted with all sorts of crooked figures. It made the beast look like an otherworldly creature. The man's outfit was made of animal hide and he was heavily armed with a hatchet, a rusty musket and a spear.

Before this rider stopped directly in front of Mastaan and Chhagan, three more tribal ruffians emerged from the dark vegetation. All were mounted on ominously painted horses. All were armed to the teeth. None of them uttered a word.

Within moments, twenty more horsemen encircled the touring party. By the time the sawaars of the D'Cruze Regiment formed a protective ring around their two female guests, they were surrounded by a hundred tribal dacoits.

And then he appeared – the warlord of Delhi's wild hinterland.

Jogi Naagar.

His black skin shone under a film of sweat. His teeth were crooked, and his ears were mauled into ugly knots as a result of years of savage wrestling. Riding an abnormally mammoth black bull in order to accentuate his self-propagated reputation of being *Yama*, the God of Death, he trudged towards Mastaan. A massive thick-sword rested on his shoulder and vicious cruelty dripped from his eyes.

'Oh ho ho... what have we here!' said Jogi in a mocking tone and a rustic dialect of Hindustani. He knew his men outnumbered the Company's sepoys by more than ten to one. 'Lost our way, have we? What do they call you... urmmm... yes... Mastaaaan?!'

Mastaan, Chhagan, Balram and Shahbaaz did not flinch one bit. They had seen and overcome significantly worse odds. But this time, to his own amazement, Mastaan was uncharacteristically anxious. For the first time in his life, he felt intensely and singularly responsible for someone's safety. While during all his battling years he had stood like a shield in front of Chhagan, Robert D'Cruze and every one of his men, somehow the weight he felt today was different. More piercing.

She was his to protect. *Only his.*

In these heavy moments of stark danger and duress, surrounded by bloodthirsty savages, Mastaan suddenly realized.

Fay was his to protect.

Fay was his.

'Look, Joginder... it is a very bad idea accosting us like this, my friend. Looks like you have forgotten what happened the last time we met,' shouted Chhagan. He wanted everyone, especially Jogi's tribesmen, to hear him.

Mastaan sighed under his breath. He was not sure if this was the best time to incite the wild animal that lurked deep inside the leathery hide of Jogi Naagar. Under normal circumstances, it was the bold and brash Mastaan who would have mocked and provoked an enemy fearlessly. But in a matter of a few hours, Mastaan's circumstances had changed radically.

Jogi was now trembling with rage. The Subedaar-Major had doubly insulted him. One, he hated being called by his real name – Joginder. As far as he was concerned, he was the dreaded bandit-chieftain 'Jogi' for one and all. Two, Chhagan had reminded him of his humiliating defeat at the hands of Mastaan - a one-sided duel, the recollection of which Jogi would have liked to bury forever.

'The intoxicating scent of white flesh seems to be driving you insane, Dubey...' hissed Jogi. 'You seem to forget that I can turn this place into a graveyard for you and your guests with a snap of my finger. This young Lalla here anyway dreams of violating a *gori mem* every night!'

He guffawed menacingly, glancing at a particularly barbaric looking youth, who in turn grinned vulgarly, then licked his frothing mouth, as if to validate his well-advertised lust. He blew a kiss looking at Fay.

The tribal collective roared in a coarse laugh.

'One more word...'

Jogi and his men could not immediately place where these words came from.

'One more word... one more impropriety from this Lalla of yours, and I promise you a graveyard of your own kind, Joginder.'

Mastaan spoke matter-of-factly. He meant every word of what he had just said. And Jogi knew this well. He knew what the widely feared Subedaar of the D'Cruze Regiment was made of.

But the young henchman of the bull-riding warlord was immature and did not know who he was facing. Jogi Naagar's plan was to surround the touring party, threaten them mildly and then permit them to leave peacefully. He hoped to saddle Mastaan and Chhagan with a favor – as a valuable investment for his own future safety. But this unplanned involvement of the brash Lalla disturbed everything. Even before Jogi Naagar could utter words to pacify the legendary Mastaan, Lalla screamed out a barrage of expletives and pulled up a massive battle-axe.

DHABBAAAAAAMM...!!

DHABBAAAAAAMM...!!

It all happened in a split second.

Faster than the eye could see, Mastaan had drawn two long muskets and fired. One of the bullets hit the unfortunate Lalla's wrist, splitting it irreparably and throwing up a squirt of crimson. The other bullet hit the spear of the man standing closest to Jogi, sending the weapon twirling and flying into the vegetation like a pin tossed from a flipping finger.

In the bat of an eyelid, Mastaan had swirled both his guns, one in each hand, in the inimitable style of the D'Cruze

Regiment's cavalry and had reloaded them. The rifle in his stronger hand was aimed straight at Jogi's forehead.

In these very split moments, all of Chhagan's men had also cocked their guns and were ready to fire. Fourteen shots from the D'Cruze Regiment meant fourteen dead men as the opening gambit for Jogi.

Jogi stared hard and deep into Mastaan's eyes. The warlord's intent was never to get into a conflict in the first place. Yet everything had gone horribly wrong.

Joginder Naagar was now burning with rage.

The next few moments were heavy with anticipation of violence by both sides, as hundreds of sweaty palms gripped sword handles and rifle butts.

But it seemed that, for now, better sense prevailed over the forest warlord.

'Ye mulaqaat udhaar rahi, Mastaan...'

'This meeting shall remain a debt, Mastaan...'

With these words, Jogi turned his bull around and slowly vanished into the jungle he had come out from.

As Mastaan led the touring group out of the forest with single-minded alertness, Chhagan could see that Fay was terribly shaken. The rapid and fiery booming of Mastaan's rifles, the splattering blood from the bandit's wrist and the brutal tension in the air had all taken a toll on Fay's gentle nerves. Chhagan decided to try and divert her attention.

As he rode up to the beautiful young girl from London, Chhagan turned towards her and spoke in a mildly humorous manner.

'Now you see why they call him that?'

Fay turned and looked at him with confused eyes. She was both scared and dazed.

'Call him what?' she asked in a crisp English accent, totally unaware of what Chhagan was talking about.

'The Gunman – Bandookbaaz...' the Subedaar-Major replied, with a low, good-hearted laugh.

It was only now that Fay broke into a smile.

'I don't like him like this,' was all she could say.

The rest of their journey was uneventful and the sawaars of the D'Cruze Regiment escorted the ladies back safely to Lieutenant Robert's bungalow.

Mastaan and Fay bid farewell to each other for the day, speaking more with their eyes. Fay nearly danced back up the stairs to her room, ecstatic at the way her heart fluttered. The Bandookbaaz could not help but smile shyly at his friends all of the remaining evening.

Another beautiful love-story had begun to blossom in the sparkling Mughal capital, home to some of the most unforgettable and haunting tales of romance.

While both Fay and Mastaan were floating on a cloud of once-in-a-lifetime love, they were unaware of a grave mistake that had been committed that day.

The dreaded Jogi Naagar had gotten to know.

He knew Mastaan's one and only weakness.

Manikarnika Tambe

Rani Mahal, Jhansi, 5th March 1857

She stood gazing out of the enormous window, with the shoulder-end of her long silken *saree* flowing in the wind like a proudly fluttering flag.

She was standing in her private meeting chambers, looking over the vast plains and hills in her territory. A land that had fallen under her care, since the demise of her husband, the late Jhansi Naresh Maharaj Gangadhar Rao Newalkar four years ago. For a few brief moments the words being spoken by her political and military guests failed to reach her.

She was lost in her thoughts – mainly of care for her people.

Every house, every hut, every temple, every mosque visible from here... has my people in it. They all look up to this palace. The people of Bundelkhand look up to me...

'Do you agree, Maharani Saahiba...?'

The marvelously sculpted dome of the Durga Mandir with hundreds of small and big saffron flags flapping from its highest *stambha* or pillar that stood proudly visible from several miles was in her line of sight. She always looked towards it to derive strength in the times of adversity.

'Manikarnika, I beg your pardon... but do you agree with this plan?'

The words rang out again.

It was only now that she paid attention to the question that was directed to her. She immediately recollected the exalted stature of her guests. It was not every day that two such illustrious men made an effort to call upon another monarch.

She turned to face them, letting go of any and every womanly softness that her face may have betrayed.

'Yes, I agree. We need to join forces and resist this tyrannical, imperial Company.

I am with you, Tantya bhai.

I thank you with all my heart for making me a part of this war, Nana Saaheb.'

She was born on the 19th of November, 1828 to Moropant and Bhagirathi Tambe in the holy city of Banaras.

Studying her *kundali* or horoscope right on the day of her birth, the high priests of Kashi had spoken. The little Manikarnika was destined to not only become a rani, a queen... but she was to leave behind an unforgettable mark on the history of Hindustan.

The time for that prophecy to come true had arrived.

The little Manikarnika from Kashi had now become the indomitable Maharani Laxmi Bai of Jhansi.

Several rulers of the many princely states of Hindustan were simmering with hate for the British. The much-despised Governor General, Lord Dalhousie, had implemented the draconian *Doctrine of Lapse* ruthlessly. Under this new, unilaterally imposed annexation law by the East India Company, no adopted child was allowed to inherit the kingdom of his father. The law undermined the fundamental right of the rulers of the princely states to choose their successors. This cold and oppressive political conduct of the East India Company not only alienated scores of princes and nawabs, but also led to a widespread sense of injustice and discontent among the people at large.

As the years passed and the might of the Company increased manifold, several provinces were annexed into British India under this callous policy. Among the first few were the kingdoms of Kittur, Kozhikode and Jalaun. After these came the prominent provinces of Jhansi, Satara, Udaipur, Tanjore, Surat, Arcot, Punjab, Nagpur, Banda and even Oudh.

As of today, Jhansi was nothing more than a vassal state for the British Company. Any day now the Company's soldiers would march into the fort of Jhansi and oust Laxmi Bai. Any resistance would mean all of Jhansi being surrounded by hundreds of Company cannons and tens of thousands of British rifles. The great Rani knew her forces stood no chance in an open war with the East India Company.

In fact, this was something every single king and nawab of Hindustan was well aware of. Which was precisely why joining forces with the impending uprising was the best and the last chance any of these rulers stood against the mighty British.

It was now or never.

'Word has come from Bakht Khan, Manikarnika. He is the commander of the Bareilly brigade and the unofficial leader of the mutinying *fauj*. The date has been decided. On the 1st of June, British garrisons and cantonments all over Hindustan will erupt in revolt, all in unison!' explained Nana Saaheb, the adopted son of Peshwa Baji Rao II and, as he liked to believe, the rightful heir to a revived Maratha confederacy.

Tantya Tope, childhood companion of both Nana Saaheb and Rani Laxmi Bai, now held the post of the commander-in-chief of Nana Saaheb's ragtag army from Bithoor (near Cawnpore). Jhansi, on the other hand, still boasted of small yet well-equipped armed forces comprising cavalry, infantry and even some artillery. It was Tantya that raised the first concern.

'But Nana Saaheb, isn't 1st of June too close? Will we be able to rally the other states and provinces in such short time? Moreover, we have only 1,200 men in our Bithoor troops as of today. This is nothing compared to the mammoth British forces that will remain loyal to the Company even after one section of the sepoys revolts. We need more time, my Peshwa!'

'There is no time, Tantya!' snapped Nana Saaheb. 'The anger of the native British sipahi is a volcano waiting to erupt! If we wait too long and miss this inferno of rage, no one will be able to uproot the firangi from India for a thousand years!'

It was at this high-pitched moment during the discussion that Laxmi Bai rose from her regal seat.

She folded her hands and spoke.

'Tantya *bhau*, you are a veteran in the matters of warfare. But I do agree with Peshwa Maharaj here. This is a tide of collective angst that we cannot afford to miss. If Delhi is going to be the final battlefield under the banner of the Mughal Emperor Bahadur Shah, so be it. If the sipahi regiments are planning to raise the flag of mutiny on the 1st of June, so be it.'

With these words she drew out her gleaming sword from its gilded scabbard and raised it high up in the air towards her compatriots.

'I pledge my life, my Jhansi and my people to the cause of freeing our maatribhoomi from the scourge of the British.

Hindvi swaraj ya mrityu!'

'Indian self-governance or death!'

Laxmi Bai never failed to inspire anyone in her graceful yet forceful presence. She was an embodiment of beauty, courage and patriotism.

It was now that both Nana Saaheb and Tantya Tope rose, drew their scimitars and raised those to join the Rani of Jhansi. They pronounced in unison.

'Hindvi swaraj ya mrityu!'

Ilahi Bakhsh

Laal Kuan, Delhi, 10th March 1857

Pulling at his richly embroidered Hyderabadi sherwani to get rid of every last wrinkle, he observed and groomed each strand of his henna-dyed beard closely in the mirror. His rose, khus and sandalwood *ittra* came from the finest perfumeries of Aligarh. His haveli was among the grandest in all of Delhi.

Ilahi Bakhsh was, after all, the father-in-law of late Mirza Fakhru, favorite but now dead son of the Badshah of Hindustan. Mirza Fakhru had died of cholera. But that was the official version. Many believed that he was poisoned in cold blood.

In his usual loud and opulent style, Bakhsh was hosting a grand *mushaira,* a congregation of celebrity poets, at his residence this evening. It was to be attended by the who's who of Delhi's elite. From various shaayars of the Mughal court to the unflappable Mirza Ghalib... from the Resident Commissioner of Delhi Simon Fraser to the very young Prince Mirza Jawaan Bakht, everyone was going to add to the glitter of the much talked-about evening.

Robert D'Cruze happened to be one of the few not-so-senior British officers that found a place in the evening's discerning guest-list. This invitation was not totally disconnected with the fact that Robert led the Company Bahadur's most fearsome regiment. Brute power attracts many friends. As was the order of the day, Lieutenant Robert walked proudly in to the sparkling haveli of Ilahi Bakhsh, accompanied by his two most able men. Upon Robert's insistence cum directive, Mastaan had shaved his usual stubble clean and looked nearly as fair as an Englishman.

Both he and Chhagan were on their best behavior.

'*Khushaamadeed*... Robert saahab,' welcomed the aging yet elegant Bakhsh, as he saw Robert D'Cruze set foot into the large courtyard that today served as the venue for the poetic gathering.

Ilahi Bakhsh's haveli was second to none in all of Delhi and Hindustan. From an intricately stone-carved entrance patio to a vast courtyard surrounded by ivory-white pillars of marble; from Mughal-style arched corridors to a beautiful *zenana* (ladies' quarters) overlooking the central atrium, the nobleman's mansion was a symbol of the golden city's architecture and prosperity.

'*As-salaamu Alaikum,* Bakhsh saahab,' said Robert, even as the suave Ilahi Bakhsh wrapped him in a light and well-practiced embrace that was reserved only for highly-placed nobles of the royal court and for influential British officers.

'These are my most trusted and brave men, Bakhsh saa'b... Subedaar-Major Chhagan Dubey and Subedaar Mastaan.'

Bakhsh nodded almost unnoticeably at the duo and gestured with his hand for Robert to take his seat. It was below the royal in-law's tall standards to even acknowledge the presence of ordinary natives. If left to him, he would have ousted every Hindustani from his small palace.

Chhagan and Mastaan now decided to blend into the crowd of guests and take full advantage of the open *maikhaana* and the delectable variety of kebabs.

'Take it easy, Mastaan. Last time you got drunk at the Metcalfe House dinner,' cautioned Chhagan, as the two friends picked up their first goblets of wine.

'You are one to preach now, are you, Subedaar saa'b? Look, fine wine doesn't suit you. It was you who threw up at *shahzaada* Mirza Mughal's mushaira. Even Robert saa'b saw you.'

'No, he did not.'

'Yes, he did.'

Before this minor debate could reach any conclusion, the two young men had promptly permitted themselves their first refill.

As the evening progressed, it swiftly turned into a spectacular display of Ilahi Bakhsh's dazzling wealth and the Dilli-wallahs' insatiable appetite for wine, food, poetry, beauty and revelry.

Once the gathering of rich nobles, famous poets and powerful Englishmen was sufficiently intoxicated with expensive wine, scented tobacco and the occasional puffs of cannabis, the task of serving liquor and melt-in-the-mouth meats was passed on from the servants of the Bakhsh household to some of the most desirable courtesans from Delhi's most coveted streets. The presence of these stunning beauties, who left no stone unturned in teasing these wealthy and powerful men with their provocative whispers, the breezy touch of their fingertips and subtle skin-show, slowly raised the tempo of the evening to a heady concoction.

Wives and other ladies accompanying the guests were not permitted in the main atrium of the mushaira. They were welcomed directly to the first-floor zenana, from where they could enjoy verses from the great poets of Delhi and also use the vantage point to keep an eye on their swaying men.

Once the host was convinced that both shaayars and their audience were warmed-up enough, the stalwart poets were invited to take their places on the finely embroidered silken mattresses laid on the floor.

Mastaan sat in one corner of the polished corridors, waiting for Chhagan to return from the kitchen tandoor with a fresh helping of *galouti* kebabs and deep-fried chicken. Despite being a few drinks into the evening, Mastaan was well aware that their place lay in the peripheries of the party. And it was this brazen exclusion that was reminding Mastaan of Chhagnu's words over and over again - about ultimately being outcasts from the real world of the Company Bahadur, no matter how much blood one spilled as its loyal servant.

Lost in these thoughts, Mastaan failed to notice the ringing sound of paayal anklets approaching him. Before he knew it, there was a ravishing young girl bending down at him with a tray of wine goblets. She made no effort to hide her raw youthful beauty teeming from the deep-cut blouse she wore. Her eyes were intoxicatingly large, and she smelled of the spiciest jasmine perfume.

Mastaan looked up, recognized her and gave the girl a tired smile.

'Uff...' she said, dramatically shutting her eyes as if enduring a sweet pain. 'Those killer lips...'

The Subedaar laughed at her melodrama. He could not deny that they knew each other from long before. From his days of reckless boisterousness.

'Look, Manglo... you are wasting your time. This house is full of fat, loaded men who will shower you with gold just for a wink. Go to them. Go make a killing!'

She brought her face closer to Mastaan's and whispered again, more endearingly than before.

'Those already-killed don't make a killing, Bandookbaaz. You slaughtered me two years ago. My soul still awaits you... for you to quench its thirst forever...'

Mastaan always enjoyed Manglo's crazy banter and her playfulness. But he did not expect what she did next.

Throwing caution to the wind, Manglo first rubbed her cheek against Mastaan's and then, with an impish giggle, bit his earlobe. The Subedaar moved away after a moment or two and held Manglo's forearms in an attempt to gently distance her from himself. But it was too late.

Someone was watching Mastaan every second from behind the first-floor stone-mesh railings of the zenana.

It was now that their eyes met.

Fay was looking straight at Mastaan from across the courtyard, a floor above.

Even in the dim nightlight, Mastaan could see clearly.

Her beautiful face was flush-red, contorted with pain.

Her eyes were brimming with tears.

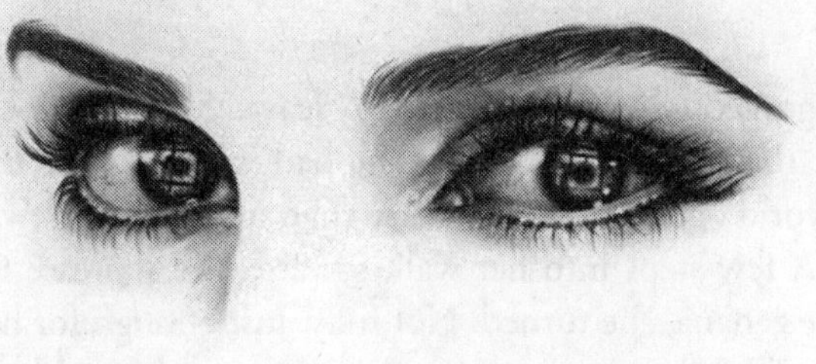

You can call me Fay

Laal Kuan, Delhi, 10th March 1857

'Manglo, please... I beg of you. There is no one who can help me here.'

As Mastaan pleaded with her to take his message across to the zenana, the famous harlot of Delhi was crumbling with amorous disbelief. Someone who pretended to be in love with a different, repulsive man every night, someone who heard cooing proposals of affection and marriage during the short-lived physical act, and someone who was used to being thrown away like a piece of worn clothing the next morning – Manglo was the closest to recognizing real love when she saw it.

'Oh, Mastaan...' she said, her fingertips covering her beautiful lips curled in awe. 'You are in love!'

'Just ask her to meet me at the terrace in ten minutes, Manglo. I will not forget this favor.'

'Uff...' she said again, her eyes twinkling under a thin film of tears and longing. 'I will take your message to the gori mem, my killer.'

The gorgeous Manglo turned to leave. She was not a day older than twenty-three, but she had witnessed far more of the world's good, bad and worse than most women twice her age. A few steps into her walk towards the staircase leading to the zenana, she turned. Not fully. Just enough for her eyes to meet Mastaan's once more, her chin touching the delicate beauty-bone of her marble-like skin.

'If you ever fail in love, Mastaan... don't forget your Manglo, okay? She will wait for you... till eternity.'

Mastaan laughed politely and in response expected to see Manglo laugh as well in her naughty playfulness. She did not. Instead, she looked into his eyes for a split moment longer, in a manner so broken that made her appear vulnerable beyond words, desirable beyond dreams.

She then vanished into the crowd of guests, making her way to the ladies' quarters on the first floor.

It took the Bandookbaaz of the D'Cruze Regiment no time to climb up the tall and numerous windows of the Bakhsh mansion, sneaking up from the back-lane of the house to reach the rooftop.

His trusted comrade, Subedaar-Major Chhagan Dubey, stood guard to ensure that no one came in the way of his friend Mastaan meeting his beloved Fay alone for the first time.

Twenty minutes passed as Mastaan paced up and down the sprawling terrace of the large house, all alone in the orange darkness, waiting for Fay to appear from the doorway that came up from the ladies' chambers. The evening was now coming to life and some of the younger shaayars had begun reciting their *kalaam* or poetic discourses. The night-sky was illuminated with oil lamps of the dusty streets of Delhi or Shahjahanabad as it was also called, and with the thousands of lanterns sparkling from the windows of homes, shops and taverns of the marvelous city. In a distance the magnificent dome of the Jama Masjid dominated the horizon.

Despite being in the melancholy trough of its steady decline since the invasion of Nadir Shah and the unspeakable genocide that followed, even now Delhi appeared to be shimmering like a golden treasure spreading out as far as the eye could see.

It was the paradoxical fate of this blessed and cursed metropolis.

To rise to the zenith of prosperity and shine like a paradise city on one day.

Only to drown in blood and burn like the ashes of *marghat* on another.

She was trembling.

Whether it was her angst at seeing Mastaan flirt with another woman, the fear of being spotted with him by the entire royal gathering, or simply the nervous excitement of being alone with her man for the first time - Fay was shivering with anxiety.

Mastaan stepped forward and took both her hands in his own. He bent towards her to look into her deep blue eyes that appeared a hypnotic silver-grey in the auburn hue of the night.

'Thank you for coming to see me, F...' said Mastaan, unsure if he could call the refined English girl by her name just yet.

She stayed quiet for a moment, slowly slipped her fingers out of Mastaan's hands and turned away, looking blankly into the cityscape.

The long-haired Bandookbaaz was now at a loss of ideas. Before he could think of what to say or do next, Fay spoke softly, still looking away.

'You can call me Fay.'

For a moment he could not grasp what she had just said, after which he broke into a quiet smile. These words came as a big relief for Mastaan.

Fay could sense what was going on in his mind. Nonetheless, he knew she was deeply upset. Even though it meant nothing to Mastaan, Manglo's act of pecking on his ears could not have looked innocent even to the most trusting onlooker. And Fay did not even know him well.

'What you saw is not what it appears to be, Fay. Yes, I knew this girl a couple of years ago. Yes, she continues to be a friend even today... but that is all. There is nothing between us!'

A moment of silence was followed by the question Mastaan was dreading.

'Have you been with her, Mastaan?'

Mastaan knew what Fay was asking. He could have lied to her. But he did not. Not to his Fay.

'Yes,' he said, with a sigh. 'But that was more than two years ago. That was when I did not even imagine someone like you will walk into my life, Fay. I don't even know what you feel for me, or whether you feel anything for me at all. Everything is different now. Just a few meetings... a few hours with you seem to have changed me forever. It is only you now, Fay. Just you.

And please don't get me wrong. I know you probably don't even love me... the way I have begun to love you, but it does not matter. I don't think I will be able to love anyone again for the rest of my...'

She turned, went up on her toes and pressed her soft lips on his.

'Shhhh...' she whispered, and put her arms around Mastaan's shoulders, caressingly gripping his beautiful hair with her fingers, gently taking his lower lip into her warm mouth.

Love Against Hate

Laal Kuan, Delhi, 10th March 1857

Fay and Mastaan sat in each other's arms on the brick floor, her head nestled on his shoulder and their fingers clasped, as they peered into the starry sky of midnight Delhi. At this moment, when their breath became one and their hearts beat in harmony, the Hindustani warrior and the young British girl let go of all their fears. They knew they came from diametrically opposite cultures, religions and social strata. The color of their skin was as different as the ways-of-life they represented.

Never in the history of the East India Company had a native commoner dared to love an English noblewoman. And yet here they were – lost in each other's touch and scent... pushing away, for just this once, the harsh realities of the world surrounding them.

There was a sudden hush followed by a cheering roar when the name of Mirza Asadullah Baig Khan was announced.

With the central atrium on the ground floor opening directly onto the terrace carrying some of the evening's glow with it, they could hear every word of the mushaira.

'Do you know who he is?' asked Mastaan.

He wanted her to know what interested him, what he liked, what he disliked... everything. Just as much he wanted to know everything that meant anything to her...her hobbies, her tastes, her interests, her fears and her dreams. Deep down Mastaan was stunned to discover an intense romantic in himself. All his life he had nurtured a self-perception that outlined the personality of a hardened warrior and a reckless maverick.

Fay had come into his life like a fragrant breeze and changed everything.

'No. Who is he?' she asked.

'You just heard his name. But he is more popularly called Mirza Nausha, or Mirza Ghalib. As I see it, he is Delhi's... maybe even all of Hindustan's greatest shaayar. Some people find his work very elitist in terms of its language. But I think he is a magician with words. He has a gift like none other.'

'Who could've known that this toughened warrior... this Bandookbaaz of the D'Cruze Regiment... had the heart of a poet?' she said, her twinkling eyes looking into his, as if discovering something new about her man every new moment. 'Will you explain to me what he says... this Mirza Ghalib?'

Mastaan smiled and nodded, as he kissed her forehead.

'Aah ko chaahiye, ik umra asar hote tak;

Kaun jeeta hai teri zulf ke sar hote tak.'

'Waah! Waah! *Subhanallah*!' the audience erupted in praise as Mirza Nausha recited the first sher of his ghazal.

Fay turned to Mastaan with the most adorable wrinkle on her forehead and childlike enquiry in her large eyes. The chaste Urdu was clearly beyond her.

Mastaan laughed at her endearing fuss-making.

I love her so much!

'In Urdu shaayari,' he began, 'the entangled or uncombed condition of a woman's hair represents her being in a state of anger or angst, targeted at her lover, of course. From what I understand, in this sher the man is imploring, albeit subtly, with his beloved that -

Every sigh of pain emanating from his heart has limited time for it to touch her, before dying into nothingness;

But by the time her anger subsides, he would be no longer alive.'

'How beautiful!' exclaimed Fay, evidently impressed by the depth of sentiment and romance. 'Sad, but beautiful.'

'And believe me, my translation is most unjust to the real beauty of Mirza's words,' clarified Mastaan, not sure if he had been able to convey the real thought of the couplet correctly even by a remote distance.

As precious minutes passed and the Mirza from Ballimaran recited more spellbinding verses, the atmosphere became surreal... more romantic than even the great poets of yore had ever described in their passionate writings.

'You know, Mastaan... I could stay here till eternity, in your arms, listening to these golden poetic verses from Mirza Ghalib, explained to me by you so lovingly. And just so you know, I will never remain angry with you for long, no matter what, as you might have just seen!'

By the time she ended her statement, Fay feigned displeasure once again, remembering the stunning native girl who could match her own beauty any day.

Mastaan knew better than to delve deeper into this discussion. Moreover, it had been over one hour since they had both been missing from the mushaira. It would not be long before Robert got alarmed and sent out a search party through the Bakhsh mansion.

'We should leave now, Fay,' he said, raising her face towards him with a finger under her chin.

'And when do we see each other again, Mastaan?' she replied, suddenly realizing that the moment to say goodbye had arrived, at least for now.

Against the silver moonlight, she looked like everything Mastaan had ever dreamed of... and far beyond.

'Very soon, my one and only Fay. I don't even know how I am going to live another day without seeing you. I guess our messengers will have to play a very active role now.'

'Messengers...?'

'Yes. Pat from your end and Chhagnu from mine. They are the only ones who can deliver letters and messages for us, don't you think?'

Fay nodded. Her eyes welled up again.

'Oh Mastaan...' was all she could say, before she fell into his arms for a long and soulful embrace.

Despite all the ghastly bloodshed and all the savage marauders, despite the ruthless invasions and the burning of its citadels to ashes, notwithstanding the rise and fall of dynasties or of monarchs, there was one inexplicable undercurrent that had kept Delhi alive through all its horrible trials.

It was the undercurrent of love.

When the envious eyes of an evil Duryodhana cast a shadow over *Indraprastha*, the most ancient city of Delhi, it was the legendary archer Arjuna's love for his beautiful consort Draupadi that stood in its way. When a Jaichand chose to betray his own motherland, it was the love of Prithviraj Chauhan and Sanyogita that spread its immortal tales across not just *Rai Pithora* but all of Hindustan. Whether it was Sultana Razia and Siddi Yaqoot or the celebrated Amir Khusrao and his sacred beloved, Delhi has always fought back.

With love against hate.

Meer Taqi Meer

Laal Kuan, Delhi, 10th March 1857

'You were fabulous, Mirza Nausha,' said Mastaan, as he bowed and greeted his celebrity shaayar.

Fay had quietly slipped back into the women's huddle. Mastaan took less than ten seconds to climb down from the second-floor terrace to get to his waiting friend. Both Mastaan and Fay were in absolute bliss, and felt like they were flying, walking a few inches above the ground. Their fingertips whiffed fragrant with each other's aroma and the words of romance spoken danced in their heads. At this time, this young couple drenched in the heady potion of love, was the happiest in the whole world.

Both Chhagan and Mastaan were now back in the central atrium of the mushaira.

'Oh ho ho... what a delight it is to see you again, Mastaan saahab!' responded Delhi's most arrogant and most loveable poet, keeping an affectionate hand on the young warrior's shoulder.

Mastaan was thrilled to note that Mirza Ghalib remembered his name.

'You remember my name, Sir... I wouldn't have expected...'

'...wouldn't have expected a senile old drunkard to remember a name... especially not when completely inebriated and rescued while throwing up, correct?' Mirza Ghalib completed Mastaan's sentence.

'Arey... that is not what I meant, Mirza Nausha...'

'Look here, young man... Bandookbaaz they call you, *janaab* Robert tells me... when you spend a lifetime tolerating the pathetic poetry of deplorable shaayars all around, drunk becomes the new normal. I am glad I did not meet you sober. I would have forgotten even your face!'

They laughed, like they always did at Mirza Ghalib's sharp and self-directed humor.

Having been brought up an orphan and tossed around in the hands of good and bad guardians during his early childhood and in his teens, Mastaan had grown up to be a good judge of people and character. He could sense that only a few inches below the outer gaiety of Mirza Nausha lay some unspeakable sorrows and fears. He could not pinpoint those yet but he could sense an ocean of pain and suffering churning inside the magnificent old shaayar.

What Mastaan did not know was that men like Mirza Ghalib were not just among the greatest poets of Delhi.

They were the city's beating heart.

And it is the heart that begins to brace itself first, when it senses something dark and ominous lurking around the corner.

Long ago it was a man named Meer Taqi Meer who could sense the impending cataclysm.

Today it was Ghalib.

To Mastaan and Chhagan's surprise, Mirza Nausha was preparing to leave.

From all the gatherings they had witnessed in the past, most only from a distance, he was never one to call it a day too soon. In fact, Mirza Asadullah had to be respectfully yet literally thrown out of most get-togethers. And yet, today he seemed to be in a rush.

In a frightened rush.

'Please allow me to see you off, Sir...' said Mastaan, as he left no opportunity to soak in the fan moment he was going through. 'You are indeed the greatest poet ever born, Mirza saahab.'

The aging yet mesmeric nobleman from Ballimaran paused for a moment and took a break from his scores of goodbyes with the rich and powerful men of the evening.

'I am not the greatest, Bandookbaaz. There has been only one legendary poet in Delhi, and only one legendary lover too. And he was the finest shaayar Dilli or Agra or Lucknow has ever seen, my dear Mastaan.'

Mastaan and Chhagan looked at each other in wonderment. They could not think of anyone who could outshine Mirza Ghalib himself.

Ghalib could see the bewilderment on the faces of his young friends. He decided to end the confusion with a sher.

'Rekhte ke tum hi ustaad nahin, Ghalib;

Kehte haiin agle zamaane mein koi Meer bhi tha.'

'You are not the only champion of poetry and writing, O Ghalib;

They say that in the olden times there was also a man called Meer.'

Mastaan and Chhagan were mesmerized hearing the flamboyant Mirza Nausha praising another of his kind with such generosity. It was not like him to do that. This told both fighters of the D'Cruze Regiment that this poet of yore must have been someone extraordinary.

They did not have to wait long. Mirza Ghalib spoke again.

'His name was Meer Taqi Meer.

The greatest lover of Agra.

The greatest poet of Delhi.

Of all time.

He perished with the city of his heart, Mastaan.

He knew it was all going to end.'

In a matter of moments, Mirza Ghalib's jovial mood had turned unnervingly somber.

As if this time it was he who knew something he was not able to share.

As if this time he was the one fated to perish.

Mirza Ghalib was in a strange haste to get out of the premises of the house. As he hurried through his greetings and hobbled over to the exit door swiftly, Mastaan followed him. Just as Ghalib was about to step out of the building, Mastaan held him gently by the elbow.

'What is the matter, Mirza Nausha? You seem to be eager to leave this evening even before you have had a few drinks. This is most unlike you,' said the fighter of the D'Cruze Regiment, in a vain attempt to make Ghalib smile.

'Yes, I am in a hurry. And if you knew what I know, you would be scurrying too.'

Mastaan kept looking into Mirza Ghalib's eyes, waiting for the maestro to say something more and explain the mysterious puzzles he was weaving with his hushed tone and now menacing demeanor.

'Run.'

That was all Ghalib said.

'Sorry... what did you say, Mirza?'

'Run away from here.

Take your beautiful white girl with you and go away...!'

With these words Mirza Asadullah Baig Khan climbed down the entrance stairs and left. As he walked a few steps ahead, he realized that Mastaan was still standing at the entrance patio, watching him leave, too dazed to say anything.

Seeing this the greatest shaayar of all time and the man who would become as immortal as the city of Delhi, spoke the fateful words… trembling with mortal fear.

'This mansion is cursed, Bandookbaaz.

This mansion… and its inhabitants… have been cursed for the last 58 years!

Ilahi Bakhsh is not a man.

He is a goblin.

Run.'

Part 2

Gayi yak-ba-yak jo hawa palat,
Nahin dil ko mere karaar hai;

- BAHADUR SHAH ZAFAR

Eye of the Blood-Storm

Married Officers' Quarters, near Metcalfe House, Delhi, 30th March 1857

Robert woke up with cold sweat.

'Robert saahab... please get up, Sir!'

He turned to look at the face of his Hindustani servant. In an instant Robert knew something was seriously amiss. His well-trained native servants would never dare wake him unless the heavens had fallen.

'What is it, Avdhesh?'

The head-servant of Robert's bungalow folded his hands and stood back. This was indication enough that he wanted the English officer to rise fully and take cognizance of the news Avdhesh was the bearer of.

Robert threw away the sweaty sheet that protected him from the mosquitoes of early-summer Delhi and took a gulp of water.

'Tell me!' he commanded.

'You have been summoned by Lord Fraser, my lord. There has been... has been a...' the head-servant hesitated.

'There has been a *what*... ?!' demanded Robert, now already on his way towards his uniform closet.

'Saahab... there has been a revolt of sorts. A lunatic of a soldier of the 34th Bengal Native Infantry opened fire on his officers yesterday, Sir. The news has just reached the Residency.'

'What...??' Robert scowled. What Avdhesh had just shared was unacceptable.

'Yes, janaab. This has something to do with the rumor of... pardon me, my lord...'

Robert was now beginning to get frustrated. He was a young, fiery and just British officer, who liked to take things head-on. Avdhesh's dilly-dally was beginning to make him angry.

'Avdhesh... you speak clearly now or get out of my room. I don't have the time for your bloody antics!' Robert yelled.

'This appears to be the beginning of something very grave, saahab,' the head-servant took the warning clearly. 'A sipahi fired at his officers at the Barrackpore chhaavani yesterday. He refused to bite into the new cartridges being commissioned, saahab. While only one or two other soldiers actively helped him, they are saying he has moved the soul of every Hindustani sipahi of the Company Bahadur, my lord.'

By now the young Robert had strapped on his sword, brushed his short hair and pulled-up his military boots.

'What do you make of it, Avdhesh?' he asked, as he loaded his Colt with six glistening bullets.

Avdhesh once again hesitated, but quickly understood that the time for diplomacy was gone.

'This was coming, Robert saahab. For months our sipahis have been restless and anxious about the new Enfield cartridges greased with pig and cow fat. But no officer from the Company Bahadur has taken this matter seriously. Even today, no one knows whether the new shells are indeed coated with this blasphemous grease or not. What else did we expect, my lord? You can take away the Hindustani's land, his home, his crop and his liberty. But when you try to take away his God... he shall never forgive you, saahab... never.'

Robert was fastening the loops of his revolver holster as he heard these words. He could not help but stop and turn to look at Avdhesh. This was the first time his loyal head-servant had spoken so openly, so fearlessly.

I must reach the Residency as soon as possible.

'Ready my horse, Avdhesh,' commanded Robert, as if nothing had happened.

But he could see.

He could see that Avdhesh was somehow not the same man anymore. His obedient servant today betrayed a glint of arrogance in his eyes.

Robert tried to divert the conversation to a more operational zone.

'So, what did you say his name was, the sepoy who mutinied yesterday at Barrackpore?'

As he turned to look at his most dependable orderly, the young British officer was stunned to see old Avdhesh's face distort into an expression of unabashed pride and unprecedented partisanship.

'Mangal,' he said, as if pronouncing the name of a great hero.

'Mangal Pandey.'

Tasbihkhana, Laal Qila, Delhi, 30th March 1857

The Emperor of Hindustan began his days early. Both age and the scorching chains of bondage - of being a puppet-king - had stolen away sleep from his old eyes a long time ago.

It was 5 am when his friend and physician Ahsanullah Khan appeared at the arched doorway of the King's prayer and reading room.

'What brings you here at this hour, Ahsanullah?' enquired Zafar. He was not particularly alarmed. It was probably again one of his princes who had tormented a commoner or robbed a merchant. Or another concubine found fooling around with one of the palace guards.

But within a moment the old King's eyes spotted a terrified yet jubilant expression on the physician's face. It was as if Ahsanullah was both mourning and rejoicing at the same time. Now this odd dichotomy worried Zafar, who slowly got up from his knees with the help of a bejeweled walking stick.

'It has begun, Jahanpanaah... just like the half-faced dervish had prophesied... it has begun!' blurted Ahsanullah.

Over the next few minutes the royal physician updated the King about the spark of mutiny in Barrackpore. He gave the Emperor a blow by blow account of the violent skirmish between the Indian sepoy and Sergeant-Major James Hewson, Lieutenant Henry Baugh and other Britishers. On being told that the brave sepoy from the 34th Bengal Native Infantry had refused to give in or get captured and had actually fired his musket upon his own chest, pulling the trigger using his toe, the Mughal monarch could not hide his glee.

'*Wallah*! What courage! What arrogance!' he exulted as if he had fought the Barrackpore cantonment battle himself. 'Now *this* is the Hindustani nerve made of steel that the firangi need to be shown, Ahsanullah!'

Ahsanullah stood transfixed in his place, shaking his head in continued disbelief.

'What is the matter, hakim?' asked Zafar. 'You don't seem very happy. Does this rebellion not mean glory for the bloodline of Timur? Is it a bad omen of some kind? Has... has this fool of a sipahi committed a horrible mistake? Will there be a sweeping British backlash? Can it mean the end of the road for us... for your King?'

'Oh, no no... Badshah *salaamat*! Not at all...' replied Ahsanullah quickly. He knew the Emperor better than most. Once again, he saw Zafar vacillate from extreme delight to dark dejection in a matter of seconds. Bahadur Shah was by far the most indecisive and dithering man the doctor of *Yunaani* (Greek) medicine had ever come across.

And yet, it was in that dark, blackwater cavern that Ahsanullah had witnessed the most jarringly resolute side of the Badshah.

Despite the physician's repeated warnings, Zafar had asked the half-faced dervish for the most impossible of wishes – in return for the most unspeakable price.

'Then what is it? What is bothering you? Speak up!'

Ahsanullah smiled and bowed.

'All I am stunned about is the swiftness with which the fateful prophecy of the half-faced man seems to be unfolding, Jahanpanaah. It was only three months ago that we stepped down to the macabre river-cave. And today a sipahi openly revolts! This cannot be a mere coincidence.'

The old Mughal grinned... broader than he had grinned in years. Ahsanullah noticed a gleam of cruel satisfaction shimmer across the King's eyes for a split moment.

He has forgotten the price he had promised to the dervish and his dark djinn.

'This fire will spread, Ahsanullah. Other chhaavanis will follow suit,' said Zafar, as he walked towards the large balcony attached to his study. Dawn had just about begun to color the navy-blue sky in the horizon orange. 'What is his name? This sipahi of the 34th Bengal?'

'His name is Mangal, Jahanpanaah,' replied Ahsanullah Khan.

'Mangal Pandey.'

The Governor General's Residence, Fort William, Calcutta, 30th March 1857

Charles Canning was as astute an administrator as he was a politician.

He did not dislike India or its inhabitants. Along with his predecessor Lord Dalhousie and the brilliant social reformer Ishwar Chandra Vidyasagar, Canning had legislated the Hindu Widows Remarriage Act of 1856. He was a social and administrative reformer at heart and wanted to transform his Indian subjects for the better. The only problem was, as per him, they were still his *subjects*.

What he did not know this morning, as he sat down for his hot bacon, baked beans and eggs breakfast, was that his grip on the subcontinent was about to be tested beyond his worst nightmare.

'Come in,' he responded to the uneven and hurried knock on the door.

'Good morning, Sir!' said his Staff Officer, sweating profusely as an outcome of the long sprint and frantic climb up the stairs to Canning's offices in the humid city.

'What is it, Wright?' enquired the Governor General, already in full dress uniform at this early hour of the day, chewing away at his full-English morning repast. His sharp features and his curly hair added to the air of aristocracy he carried about himself.

'Some disturbing news from Barrackpore, I'm afraid, my Lord,' replied Major Wright.

'Go on,' said Canning, still not looking up.

'There has been an incident of mutiny, Sir. A sepoy named Mangal Pawndy of the 34th BNI opened fire on his officers yesterday. It's once again the bloody cartridges, Sir.'

There was a moment of silence. Lord Canning gestured to an orderly, who poured steaming Assam tea into his cup.

Confused at seeing no reaction from the Governor General, Major Wright cleared his throat and asked directly.

'What are my orders, Sir? This is clearly an act of mutiny that cannot be taken lightly.'

'None of that is for you to decide or to comment on, William,' replied Canning firmly.

'Yes, Sir.'

'Please inform General Anson. I am certain he will take all the necessary measures to address this behavioral anomaly.'

Behavioral anomaly? This is a bloody mutiny!

'Yes, Sir. Please allow me to take leave of you. Good day, Sir.'

Major William Wright saluted the Governor General and left the large sunlit room furnished with thick mahogany.

As soon as he left the room, Canning threw his knife and fork into the delicate china on his long table with a clang.

This is a bloody mutiny!

And old Anson is not going to be able to do anything about it.

What was the name Will mentioned?

Mangal.

Mangal Pawndy.

Rani Mahal, Jhansi, 30th March 1857

The beautiful Rani clutched one of her hands with the other, to stop it from trembling.

'But Shivani... this is too early! Everything will be lost if we lose all the coordination between the various forces of the Uprising...'

Maharani Laxmi Bai harbored no illusions. She knew that even with the combined strength of all the mutinying chhaavanis and the forces of all the rebelling princely states, defeating the British was still going to be an uphill task. The East India Company was a well-oiled, brutally-trained and vastly-funded war colossus. If the armies of the Uprising were to get fragmented, they did not stand a chance.

'But Manikarnika *didi*, the British must have received the jolt of their lives! If one single sipahi of the Company Bahadur can inflict such a devastating blow that the whole of Hindustan is talking about it, imagine what a hundred thousand will do!'

Laxmi Bai smiled at the naivety of her childhood friend. All she could see now was the inevitable demise of the grand Uprising that Nana Saaheb, Tantya Tope and she had envisioned along with scores of other nawabs and *riyaasats*. She could picture her Jhansi surrounded by tens of thousands of troops in red tunics. She could almost hear the thunderous pounding of several hundred British cannons.

She knew it was all over. One bullet fired too early was going to change the fate of Bhaaratvarsha forever.

She wiped her tears using one end of her flowing Banarasi saree.

'Who is this silly brother of mine, who could not wait for his sister to raise her banner?' she asked, half laughing, part crying. 'What is this immortal warrior's name, Shivani?'

Blessed would be the man whose name gets enquired about by none other than the *mardaani* of Bundelkhand.

'I'm not sure, didi. But I heard the name Mangal.'

Manikarnika Tambe smiled and rested her glance on the Durga Mandir once again.

'Mangal... indicates a pious, positive beginning,' she said. 'What is his full name, Shivani?'

'Mangal Pandey, didi.'

D'Cruze Regiment Barracks, Delhi Cantonment, 30th March 1857

'Get up...' said Chhagan, his eyes red with tears and deranged lust for retribution. 'Get up, Mastaan baba!'

'Let me sleep, Chhagnu... we drank so much last night. How on earth are you up already, bhai...?' protested Mastaan, pulling his coarse bedsheet over his head.

Subedaar-Major Chhagan Dubey was left with no patience this morning. The news that had come from Barrackpore had pierced his heart to shreds. But his real worry was Mastaan. He did not know how to break the crushing news to his beloved and volatile Bandookbaaz.

'*Utth jaa*, Mastaan... get up, Mastaan' was all he could say, before his voice cracked hoarse with sorrow.

It was now that the long-haired gunman of the D'Cruze Regiment raised his head.

'What is the matter, Chhagnu?' he asked, throwing away the sheet and noticing his friend's distraught face for the first time.

'They are going to hang him, Mastaan.'

'Hang whom, Chhagnu...?' asked Mastaan, irritated and impatient.

'They are going to hang Mangal, my friend!

They are going to hang your brother... our brother...

They are going to hang Mangal Pandey!'

The Murder at Barrackpore

Dhanbad (modern-day Jharkhand), Bengal Presidency, 8th April, 1857

In the pre-dawn darkness, through the wilderness of the erstwhile kingdom of Magadh, the two riders galloped at the speed of the wind.

While the rest of the D'Cruze Regiment had marched towards the chhaavani at Ambala for exercises in the new Enfield musketry, Lieutenant Robert had permitted Subedaar-Major Chhagan Dubey and Subedaar Mastaan to ride eastwards in the other direction. They had told him they were riding to Awadh to visit Chhagan Dubey's seriously ailing grandmother. But that was not the truth. Much as they disliked being dishonest with their able commander, both Chhagan and Mastaan knew they could not have revealed their real destination to Robert. Nor their real intent.

For their destination was Barrackpore.

And their intent was a daring prison-break and rescue of Mastaan's much-loved cousin.

For seven days and seven nights they had been riding incessantly, changing horses wherever possible. They knew time was running out fast. Mangal had been court-martialed the previous day and had been sentenced to death. The penalty was slated to be carried out on the 18th of April, just ten days away. The deadly duo of Mastaan and Chhagan had sworn to attack the Barrackpore cantonment jail in the darkness of the night and ride away with Mangal. They hoped to get some support from the 5th Company of the Bengal Native Infantry. They were relying on the camaraderie of the Hindustani soldiers who were witness to Mangal's incredible bravado and were now seething with anger against their British masters.

Mangal had opened fire on two British officers from behind the station-gun of the quarter-guard building adjacent to the Barrackpore chhaavani parade ground. He had then taken them on singlehandedly with his sword. He succeeded in dismounting one officer and wounding the other grievously. While none of his compatriots had come to his rescue, they had tried to help him passively by not carrying out the orders of the British officers. When finally outnumbered, Mangal had attempted to shoot himself. He got wounded and his uniform tunic caught fire. But the British had succeeded in apprehending him alive.

He had not even tried to defend himself in the military court and had accepted full responsibility for his actions. In these circumstances, the two fighters from the D'Cruze Regiment knew, the hanging would not be further delayed. The British would try to set an example for all native soldiers by killing Mangal Pandey as soon as possible.

Even now, they were underestimating the ruthless cunning of the Company Bahadur.

They cantered into Barrackpore by late evening of 8th April. To their amazement, the town seemed dead. The dusty roads were all deserted, the opium joints shut and even the street-hawkers were missing.

After knocking on several doors and being turned away, Mastaan and Chhagan finally met a man they could identify as a soldier in the Bengal army. He sat at the foot of a closed opium outlet, smoking cannabis. This gave some hope to the travelers from Delhi.

'Brother, why is the town so gloomy this evening?' asked Chhagan, as he squatted next to the smoking soldier.

The intoxicated man turned to look at Chhagan with woozy eyes.

'Hanged him!' he suddenly burst out. 'The bastard firangi hanged our Mangal!'

With these words he broke into sobs and hiccups.

Mastaan stepped forward and kept a consoling hand on the man's shoulder. Clearly the cannabis had made the sipahi lose track of time and day. The hanging was still a good ten days away.

'Yes, they are planning to hang him, brother. But let us not lose hope. Can you tell us which prison he is incarcerated in? And can you introduce us to some senior Hindustani officers of the 5th Company?'

The bhaang was not the culprit here.

'Are you not listening to me...?' the crying man retorted, brushing away Mastaan's hand from his shoulder. 'They have hanged him! This very morning! The scoundrels declared a later date of 18th April. But they surreptitiously killed Mangal ten days in advance. Why else do you think the whole town mourns??

You are late, my brothers. Mangal Pandey has already walked the path of martyrdom!'

Mastaan wept like a baby, unable to come to terms with this loss.

For decades and centuries to come, Mangal Pandey would be remembered by every Indian as the greatest soldier of the first war for independence from the British. The astrologer who had studied his palm was absolutely right. Mangal had indeed become immortal and his name would shine like a beacon till eternity.

But for Mastaan, he was just a younger brother.

'I could not save him, Chhagnu... we could have reached a day earlier. If we had come just one day sooner, I would've saved him...'

Chhagan Dubey sat next to his friend, one arm around him, permitting him to grieve.

'We did not know, Mastaan. We rode day and night. There was no way we could have reached sooner. Who could tell that the villains will play such lowly...'

'There is a way to avenge, Mangal... if that helps,' interrupted the soldier with the bhaang.

In an instant Mastaan turned to look at the man, his eyes on fire!

'And what would that be, brother...?' hissed the Bandookbaaz, his voice low and his pitch tenser than what Chhagan had ever heard before.

'We all loved him,' continued the partially intoxicated soldier from Barrackpore. 'But the fear of British backlash held us back. Only one man among a thousand plus soldiers of the 34th helped Mangal that day. He defied the orders of the English officers and stood his ground. Today we all wish we had done what he did. Today we all want to hang like him.'

'Who was he, brother?' asked Mastaan, waiting impatiently for the part that promised vengeance.

'His name is Ishwari Prasad. He did not leave Mangal's side till the very end. He will also be hanged for treason and is no less a martyr. But the painful reality is that while Mangal will be remembered by one and all, no one will recall the sacrifice of Jamadaar Ishwari Prasad,' the soldier lamented, the effect of the bhaang slowly diminishing.

'I am sure the pages of history will bring him back sooner or later, and not allow him to fade away into oblivion. For now, tell me how I can avenge the killing of my brother. I will not be able to show my face to my *poorvaj*, to my ancestors, if I do nothing now. Mangal loved me... he must have waited for me! He must have counted the hours... thinking his Mastaan dada will come...'

Mastaan once again broke into tears, biting his hand to retain his anger within him, for it to fester enough for him to make someone pay dearly. With his life.

'Shaikh Paltu! He is the man who betrayed Mangal Pandey. He is the one who helped Baugh and Hewson by grabbing Mangal from behind and giving the Englishmen time to regroup and reload. Just so you know, as a reward for his loyalty, they have promoted Paltu to the rank of Havaldar in the Bengal Army. The 34th Bengal is being disbanded on the 6th of May anyway.'

There was no doubt or hesitation in Mastaan's mind. He turned to his best friend and stated matter-of-factly.

'We have to kill that traitor Shaikh Paltu, Chhagnu. We have to kill him.'

'Havaldar Paltu...?'

A voice rang out as Havaldar Shaikh Paltu walked back to his new and well-guarded quarters in the chhaavani. He was *persona non grata* for the entire 5th Company and more. But all he needed to do was to bide time. The entire 34th Bengal Native Infantry was going to be shamed and disbanded in a few days. After which he would live and prosper under the protection of the Company Bahadur.

Shaikh Paltu looked around in the dwindling light of dusk. Two men appeared from behind the cantonment boundary wall. One of them, a striking looking warrior with long hair and sharp features, carried two swords.

'What do you want?' demanded Paltu, instantly realizing that the two men were not friends.

For several days Mastaan and Chhagan had followed Shaikh Paltu. After confirming the bhaang-inflicted soldier's version with several other eye-witnesses who were present on the 29th of March, the two fighters from Delhi were convinced they were after the right man.

Mastaan threw one of the swords towards Shaikh Paltu.

'Pick it up. I will not attack you from behind your back, like you did with Mangal Pandey. Pick up the weapon, Paltu.'

The Havaldar bent down and gripped the scimitar in his hands. He was a trained soldier of the East India Company and a veteran at that. He was not one to cower away from a fight.

But he tried to reason with them first.

'Why do you want to kill me? Just because I betrayed Mangal?' he asked, looking straight into the eyes of both his assailants, without even a hint of remorse.

'*Just because I betrayed Mangal?* Did you just say that, you coward?' snapped Chhagan, ready to pull out his short musket and ending the show for the day. But he knew it was Mastaan who needed the balm of Shaikh Paltu's blood on his gashed and bereaved soul.

'What was I supposed to do, brothers? If I had not captured Mangal, the British would have shot or hanged me by his side, like they are doing to poor Ishwari. Now that I did apprehend Mangal, you are here to murder me. What choice did I have? I was a dead man either way.'

Mastaan was in no mood for a conversation. He could only remember the face of his brother. Blurred memories flashed in front of his eyes, reminding him of the few happy childhood days he had spent with his uncle and his younger brother. He walked forward, raising his sword towards Paltu's throat.

The Havaldar had fought many battles. Convinced that he had no alternative but to fight his way out of this juggernaut, he yelled out a battle-cry and charged at Mastaan.

Despite his several years on the battlefield, Paltu had never fought an adversary as formidable as the Bandookbaaz of the D'Cruze Regiment.

Mastaan fell on one knee to avoid the slashing of Paltu's sword, held and twisted the Havaldar's fighting wrist in an action as swift as the slithering of cobra, and slit open Paltu's throat with a single strike of his own blade... opening the man's jugular into a red fountain.

It was all over in a matter of seconds.

Mangal Pandey had been avenged...

But when has vengeance ever heralded peace?

The mass slaughter of human beings, both white and brown, was only just beginning.

The Last Laugh

Married Officers' Quarters, near Metcalfe House, 29th April 1857

As soon as Robert entered the bungalow, he was greeted by Fay, who rushed towards him and wrapped her arms around her brother. She had been alone in the house with Pat for over three weeks now. And what she could share with no one, but her childhood friend was that even Mastaan had not met her for the entire month. Not before leaving. Not even after the D'Cruze Regiment had marched back into the Delhi cantonment earlier this morning.

Ever since Robert had lost his wife to cholera two years ago, he had drowned himself in the matters of his Regiment. Fay had been sent to Shimla, so she could be looked after well by Robert and Fay's aunt Margaret or aunt Maggie. But now that she was back in Delhi, the siblings depended on each other immensely. Robert loved Fay like a daughter, and Fay adored her older brother.

'Alright, alright... I am back now,' laughed Robert as Fay refused to let go of him. 'You can spare my ribs!'

Fay squeezed him a wee bit harder before loosening her grip. She was a delicate flower anyway. Robert, Fay and Patricia shared a good warm laugh.

The last laugh that this house was ever going to hear.

'It is all a bloody mess, to be honest, Fay,' said Robert, as he cut himself a large slice of ham.

'Behrampore, Ambala, Agra, Barrackpore, Allahabad... every garrison is on fire,' he continued, as he hungrily stuffed his mouth with the meat, getting a home-cooked meal after weeks of Ambala officers' mess food. 'Goddamn the parliamentarians who have decided to save cost on shells or the bloody evangelists who want to convert all of Hindustan to Christianity... none of them have any idea about the complexity of the Indian socio-religious fabric.'

'So, what now, Robert? How will this fire get doused? After all, the native soldiers are as much a part of the East India Company as any European officer or soldier,' enquired Fay.

'Well, it should not last too long, as I see it. I have sent a petition to the Resident Commissioner to waive off the mandate of the greased cartridges for my Regiment. I am sure soon most Regiment commanders would send in similar requests. Once the cartridges are withdrawn, there should not be any reason to worry. I am waiting for Mastaan and Chhagan to join back their duties, after which I will initiate this undertaking.'

Fay bit her lip.

'Mastaan and Chhagan were not in Ambala with you?' she asked casually, busy peeling a melon for the table. Her heart was pounding like a steam engine.

'No... no they were not. Both of them rode out to Lucknow to visit Chhagan's granny, who is not well apparently. But they asked me for a fortnight of leave, and it has been four weeks already.'

'How irresponsible of them,' quipped Pat with a silent giggle, who was quietly sipping on a hot chocolate all this while. She was immediately rebuked by a momentary glare from Fay, who could hear nothing against her Mastaan anymore.

'Not quite, Pat dearest... they are the most reliable and responsible set of men one can ask for. I can bet my life on them. Mastaan, for that matter, has saved my life literally half a dozen times by now. Something must be amiss. They would not skip reporting back on duty just like that. And God, did I miss them both during the madness in Ambala!'

'What madness, Robert?' asked Fay. She needed a diversion to prevent Robert from noticing her blushing cheeks at the mere mention of Mastaan.

Robert was quiet for a minute or two. He then spoke pensively.

'It appears to be a sepoy unrest beyond just the greased shells from Calcutta. We, the Company Bahadur, have clearly lost our way somewhere, Fay. Our native soldiers are not sub-optimal in any way. Whether it was the Carnatic Wars in the previous century, the historical battle of Seringapatam or the great Afghan War a few years ago, Hindustani sepoys have fought and bled for the Company like no other warring community. And these people, who have laid the foundation of the Company's empire with their sweat and blood, today lead the lives of low-grade laborers. Somehow the bond that kept the English officers and their Indian soldiers connected for one hundred years and more has been broken. The haughtiness of the young British officers is shockingly evident. That trouble-making preacher, Padre Jennings, is making matters worse by his proselytization activities. Without consciously planning to do so, we seem to be hurting the Indian sepoy economically, socially and religiously.'

Fay and Pat were listening carefully. They had not imagined the relations between the East India Company and its own native army to be so complex.

'All this has to be a big mistake,' Robert continued, as he closed his meal with a hot cup of tea. 'The native army of the Company is enormous. Over one hundred and fifty thousand armed sepoys are enlisted with the Bengal Army alone. Together they are a fighting behemoth! I saw their sheer muscle this time in Ambala. There was widespread arson and rioting, and the Company could do nothing about it. I shiver to imagine the consequences if this unrest spreads across the entire native army.

If that happens, Heaven forbid, not a single white man will live to tell the tale.'

'You and Pat must leave for Shimla. Or maybe even Calcutta, Fay,' Robert insisted.

'Absolutely not!' was Fay's response.

Robert had made up his mind about sending Fay and Pat off to safety while riding back towards Delhi. Something, perhaps a seasoned soldier's instinct, was telling him that a menacing storm of violence was clouding over Delhi.

Robert was right.

And wrong.

He had no idea of the scale of barbarism and brutality that Delhi was soon to be engulfed in.

'There are hundreds, perhaps thousands of English families residing in Delhi. They are not leaving the city. And you have told me yourself so many times that we are surrounded by British garrisons on all sides of Delhi! You are being paranoid. And even if you aren't, I am not leaving you here, Robert.' repeated Fay.

'Don't be silly Fay. Your presence is going to make no difference to my safety. You are not a soldier. On the other hand, knowing that Pat and you are safe in Shimla or in Fort William will be an enormous relief for me.'

But Fay was adamant. No doubt she hated the idea of leaving Robert behind, but there was another reason for her to stay on in Delhi. She could not tell Robert, not just yet – that she could not live without Mastaan. If Mastaan was going to be in Delhi even when it went up in flames, she would be by his side.

Robert tried and tried.

But Delhi had its own way.

Those it loved the most – it did not let leave.

The fate of Delhi and its inhabitants was ominously intertwined.

The Riders from Meerut

Bridge of Boats, Yamuna Riverbank, Delhi, 11th May 1857

Dawn had just broken.

They were now only a few miles away from Delhi. The ride back from Barrackpore seemed never-ending. Vendetta has great appeal and suction when unquenched, but invariably it offers little respite to the soul of the avenger. It only deforms and blackens it.

Mastaan had found no peace after killing Shaikh Paltu. In fact, he was in a miserable state. The loss of his brother combined with the one-sided duel with Paltu were making him nauseous.

The words of Havaldar Paltu were haunting Mastaan over and over again.

'What choice did I have? I was a dead man either way.'

What choice did he have?

He was just being loyal to the Company. Only days ago, I was lashing out at Chhagnu and Bakht Khan, rebuking them for their animosity towards the Company Bahadur, while brandishing my own loyalty like a medal of honor. And here I am today. One personal loss was all it took to blind me with rage and make me murder a Havaldar of the East India Company! What about the millions of my countrymen who lost their homes, their livelihoods and their loved-ones as a result of the brutality of the British? Was Chhagnu right all along?

What about Paltu's wife and children? Why are they paying a price?

What choice did I have?

It was Chhagan who started a conversation to pull Mastaan out of his deepening quagmire of pain and guilt. In recent years, the Bandookbaaz had cut-down hundreds of enemy troops in battle without a trace of penitence. But here he was, unable to accept the blood of someone who might just have been an innocent man trapped in circumstances, on his hands. And it was this pronounced sense of morality, of right and wrong in Mastaan that won him not just the love of Chhagan and the other fighters of the D'Cruze Regiment, but also their unquestioned respect.

'You see what I have been talking about, Mastaan? The differences between the Company Bahadur and the Hindustani soldiers are now irreconcilable. You have heard what has been happening at Ambala. Who would've expected that our own sawaars would torch cantonment buildings? The unrest and intense dissatisfaction of tens of thousands, in fact lakhs of sipahis is clear and visible, and yet the Company is doing nothing about it. Do we not matter at all, Mastaan baba? Does our religion mean nothing to them? Look at what they did to Mangal. He did not kill anybody. Shouldn't they have shown some kind of mercy just to pacify the army? But no... they consider themselves to be a superior race altog...'

Even before Chhagan could complete his sentence, a thick cloud of dust began to mushroom up from the horizon. Veteran soldiers as they were, both Mastaan and Chhagan could make out this was a sizeable force of cavalry approaching.

'Who could this be?' muttered Mastaan, straining his eyes to catch a glimpse of the banner accompanying the incoming army. 'Maybe it is the Company's troops returning from some other chhaavani...'

'Hmm... could be,' replied Chhagan. 'They are coming from the direction of Meerut, from across the Bridge of Boats over the Jumna. But why would they be charging at galloping speed? Whoever they are, they seem to be in a serious hurry to reach the Kashmiri Gate.'

Without any further discussion, the two tired and dusty warriors from the D'Cruze Regiment spurred on their horses and sped towards the walled city of Delhi.

The grotesque venom of primal human hate spreads faster than the raging flames of a fire-spewing dragon.

In a matter of days, Hindustan had begun to erupt like a volcano, like a long-suppressed barrel of live dynamite.

It all began with Meerut, one of the largest Company garrisons only forty miles away from the Laal Qila. The news of the one-man revolt at Barrackpore had spread like wildfire across all British cantonments. One century of oppression, racism, brutality and conceit had to pay its price. On the 10th of May, the Indian soldiers of the 3rd Bengal Light Cavalry stationed at Meerut chhaavani took up arms against their British officers. Over 2,500 native sepoys erupted in revolt, killing their European superiors, burning their bungalows and even murdering civilian women and children. They were soon joined by the 11th Bengal Native Infantry as well. The frenzy of the revolt then spread to the bazaars of Meerut, where crowds gathered and killed off-duty British officers.

Late in the night of the 10th of May, the Indian soldiers from Meerut marched towards Delhi. By the time they reached the outskirts of the Mughal capital, it was early in the morning of 11th May 1857.

Mastaan and Chhagan had witnessed the first wave of rebelling soldiers riding into the city of Delhi.

This was to be day one of the long and fierce battle that lay ahead, with the walled city as its epicenter.

'Tilange aur Purabiye'

Delhi, 0600 hours, 11th May 1857

Delhi woke up to scenes of widespread chaos and mass-panic.

It appeared as if a million horsemen had stormed through the gigantic gates of Delhi and had taken over the entire city.

Commotion was rampant on the streets and it took the Dilli-wallahs some time to figure out who the thousands of riders pounding through its roads and lanes were! As the morning progressed, some of the residents of the city began to welcome the Meerut mutineers with enthusiasm, offering them sweets, vegetables, *roti* and drinking water. The rumor of the green-turbaned riders sent by Allah soon spread across both the Muslim and Hindu neighborhoods of the city. Hundreds of people began to claim to have seen that as the riders from Meerut entered the city, their advance guard comprised divine warriors wearing green headgear and riding giant camels. As the handful of British sepoys guarding the gates tried to halt the advance of the rebel cavalry, the divine warriors were heard to have mysteriously vanished, paving the way for the Meerut riders to cut down the bleak British resistance with easy beheadings.

It was Shahbaaz who met Mastaan and Chhagan near *Barfkhaana,* the Emperor's ice factory.

'We were waiting for you both. Where have you been? The city is on fire! Bungalows of British officers are being attacked. Many of them have been slaughtered already!' Shahbaaz rattled out his words without pausing.

'Slaughtered by whom, Shahbaaz?' asked Mastaan, as the trio rode towards Metcalfe House.

'*Tilange aur Purabiye,*' replied Shahbaaz. 'Tilangas and Purabiyas, as the people of the city are calling them. Basically, by the rebel army from Meerut.'

During the early years of the East India Company, a large section of the native army was recruited from the Telangana region of southern India. Hence the name 'Tilanga'. Later on, a majority of sepoy recruitments shifted to the Awadh region as well as parts of Bihar, which lay towards the East or *purab* of the Mughal capital. Therefore, the terms *Tilanga* and *Purabiya* became common parlance to refer to the soldiers of the great mutiny.

As they galloped through packed roads and crowded by-lanes, they had only one immediate concern in mind – the safety of Robert D'Cruze and his family.

Mastaan was riding furiously, the dry air making his lips and throat parch. He was frantically trying to reach Fay as fast as he could. First the urgency to rescue Mangal and then the mad desire to avenge him had kept Mastaan away from her, much to his consternation and helplessness. Every moment of every day he had missed her. But each time he thought of Fay, he felt a sharp stab of self-reproach. As if he was being selfish by permitting her to enter his guilt-stricken heart. As if he were betraying Mangal.

Never did he imagine that he would return to her under such trying circumstances, with his beloved city on fire. He had to reach her. He had to reach Fay before anyone else did - even if it meant he had to fight through a thousand men.

The whole city was deafeningly noisy and excessively dusty today – too many martial horses galloping, un-officered paltans of loud-mouthed soldiers gallivanting through the streets, sacks of looted grain being dragged away into carts, people running helter-skelter to save themselves and their homes, large mobs shouting anti-British slogans and rich merchants being thrashed mercilessly.

And yet, the most ominous occurrence by far was the billowing of black smoke from the chhaavani area.

'They are setting the residential bungalows of the British on fire. Why are these men attacking civilians? What is the matter with them?!' yelled Chhagan, as he rode shoulder to shoulder with Mastaan.

Mastaan looked at Chhagan for a brief moment and shook his head as if to say - *I told you so.* When Chhagan had confidently stated that his own countrymen would never stoop to violence again women and children, he had forgotten. That when a mob-frenzy takes over, humans are all the same. This naturally weak primate animal, scared and subdued in normal circumstances, civilized due to the need for survival, never missed a chance to erupt with its millennia-old suppressed lust for being a predator – in the most degraded and cruel manner possible.

Chhagan was silent for the next few moments. He realized he had grossly underestimated the fury and insanity of a movement that was to be steeped in violence. It had been barely two hours since the Meerut forces had entered Delhi, and already the screams of death and destruction from the British quarters had begun to fill the heavy air.

He had waited for this day. A brutal end to the rule of the devious mercantile Company was written on the wall for months now. But despite all his hate for the firangi and his deep desire for a free Hindustan, Chhagan knew what Fay meant to Mastaan. He knew that Robert D'Cruze was a fine young man. Pat was as innocent as a child. They all had to be protected at all cost.

While Chhagan was lost in his tense thoughts, Mastaan suddenly signaled for them to stop, his own horse neighing majestically at the abrupt halt. From atop his restless and spinning mount, the Bandookbaaz spoke rapidly.

'Look Chhagan, I will ride to Robert saab's aid. Shahbaaz and you should go and round up our men. We have to assemble them at one place before they all scatter and we lose track of them in this chaos. Looks like we are going to need all the guns and all the swords we can gather today, my friend.'

'There would be a mob outside their house soon, Mastaan. These tilangas appear to be thirsty for white blood. But more than them, it is the rogue elements of every galli and mohalla that seem to be the real miscreants.'

Mastaan nodded in full agreement with the Subedaar-Major.

'You are absolutely right, Chhagnu. I just saw that kidnapper Babban, whom we had put behind bars a few months ago for the *kotwal*, walking amongst the mutineers. This means the prisons have been broken and criminals are on the loose!'

For a moment the three of them surveyed their surroundings with growing anxiety. Things were turning for the worse with every passing minute.

'I will need to reach Leftinant saahab's house as quickly as I can,' said Mastaan decisively, not willing to leave anything to chance when it came to Fay.

'But Mastaan... you are going to need Shahbaaz and me with you. The attacking horde is too large... in the thousands. You cannot take on an entire mob on your own, brother!'

Mastaan was unfazed by the warning, well founded as it was.

'Just gather the men and reach me soonest, Chhagan. But I must ride to them now!'

Chhagan nodded as he grasped the worrying urgency in Mastaan's voice.

In the next moment, the Bandookbaaz changed the direction of his horse and dashed into the narrow back-lane of an old residential neighborhood, the clopping hooves of his mount echoing as loudly as musket-fire.

As he began to gallop away, a voice called out to him from behind. It was Chhagan.

'Mastaan baba... I was wrong. If there is one man I know who can fight a mob all by himself – it is the Bandookbaaz of my Regiment!'

Mastaan grinned, shook his head and bolted forth. Chhagan's lively smile, his never-say-die attitude and his boundless confidence in Mastaan seldom failed to brighten the legendary Gunman's spirit.

Thanking the Gods, Mastaan entered the compound of Robert's residence. It was all quiet here, although it was evident that all the Indian servants, guards and orderlies had fled. Only a few houses away, large hordes of the Meerut sepoys were torching European homes. Taking advantage of the mayhem, local criminals and gangs of hooligans were using the opportunity to butcher every white-skinned person they could lay their hands on – all with just the petty motive of looting their burning homes clean.

What alarmed Mastaan was that the mob did not comprise just the 3rd Bengal Light Cavalry from Meerut.

It had faces that Mastaan recognized personally. It had faces of his friends.

Soldiers from the Delhi regiments had slowly begun to join forces with the rebels.

As Mastaan's heavy cavalry boots made the wooden steps creak, the front door of the bungalow swung open and Lieutenant Robert emerged from inside the house, prepared to open fire. He was carrying a loaded rifle. His Colt revolver was stuck into his belt, ready to be drawn at a moment's notice. He was even armed with a *talvaar*, that was strapped to his waist. All alone with two frightened girls in the house, Robert D'Cruze had equipped himself to take on a hundred men.

'Oh Mastaan...!' the young Britisher exclaimed, not hiding his relief in any manner, his voice hoarse with unexpected reprieve.

'Where have you been, my Bandookbaaz?!'

As Mastaan stepped forward and the two fine men fell into each other's embrace like a pair of old friends, Fay stood watching from the staircase inside. Her eyes could not hold back the stream of warm, comforted tears.

Where have you been, my Bandookbaaz?!

Curse of the Writhing Tiger

Delhi, 0630 hours, 11th May 1857

'Why do you not die, you pathetic old scoundrel... ?!' screamed the tall, towering man.

Despite his attempted display of anger, he appeared to be pitifully feeble in front of the otherworldly power he stood facing.

Ilahi Bakhsh was fair, handsome and muscular. And yet he stood trembling, sweating and petrified in front of the crumbled and crooked old figure that lay a few steps away.

The 99-year-old ruin of the living body of Muntasir Bakhsh looked nothing more than a blob of black coal-tar squirming on the floor. It guffawed demonically in a mad hiss... in the tragic manner of a soul condemned to insufferable guilt and excruciating agony till the end of time.

They were in the tehkhaana of the Bakhsh mansion. No one in Delhi knew about the horrifying curse of the dying, writhing

Tiger that this outwardly happy-looking haveli bore on its dark conscience. Its time had come. The bleeding, thrashing Tiger's last prophecy had spoken about this terrible hour.

And a man buried alive had never left for the realm of the dead.

'*Haarh... haarh... haarh...*' laughed the black, coughing, wriggling figure, almost blending into the blackness of the early morning corner shadows.

'They thought the old conjurer was dead...;

Before they knew... their fort was Red...!'

'Haarh... haarh... haarh...'

The basement of this grand mansion was opulent in every sense. Long galleries with finest of marble floors were dully illuminated by the gentle light of the summer dawn. For several meters one could see the regal portraits of the ancestors who once lived in this massive haveli.

Ilahi Bakhsh looked every bit royal himself, yet he paled in front of the men that peered into the onlooker's eyes from the haunted paintings - looming over the medieval family cellar. Each painting seemed to be living, breathing... *suffering*.

But the most dominating persona among all the noblemen of the Bakhsh *khaandaan* that found a place in the series of portraits was that of Ilahi's grandfather.

Muntasir Bakhsh.

His eyes could tear into the stony bosom of a thick-hide dragon and his pride could put the Sun to shame.

But this portrait was somewhat of an aberration.

It was the only painting that had two men in it.

A Muslim nobleman... Muntasir Bakhsh himself in the prime of youth, totally unrecognizable given the horrendous form he lay breathing in today.

And a striking young British officer.

The painter had done intricate justice to the presentation of these sparkling men. The turban of Muntasir dazzled with precious jewels even in paint. The colors of the work of art displayed every carving of the arch above the men's heads in all its finesse. So much so that even the name of the British officer was visible on his uniform badge.

It spelt the name John McGowen.

'Stop it! Stop it! Stop it!' screamed Ilahi Bakhsh, now unable to withstand any more of the half-faced dervish's verbal poison.

Greed, sin, betrayal, lust... they never depart without leaving a lasting, weeping and bleeding stain on the soul of the perpetrator. And when the sin committed is not just against one single human being but against the cardinal rules of life and death, such unspeakable, ghastly acts that meddle with the forbidden boundaries between the living and the dead, the atonement of such dark evil is passed on to the wrongdoer's doomed bloodline. The timeless cosmic law of *rnanubandhan* or *the eternal bondage of debt*, never fails to cast its eternal shadow - condemning generations to a morbid, otherworldly plague.

Such unpardonable sinners, whom even nature and creation had forsaken to the realms of the undead, were called *pishaacha* or *brahmaraakshasa* in the ancient Hindu scriptures. Some accomplished Sufis and dervishes of Dilli called them *djinns*.

The Seventh Burning of Delhi

Delhi, 0630 hours, 11th May 1857

'It is just the two of us against more than five hundred of them...' said Robert.

The initial greetings were done away with quite quickly. The gravity of the worsening situation far outweighed the need for all niceties. Mastaan and Fay could only exchange a glance or two, but for now those were enough to make both their forlorn souls feel the healing touch of a messiah.

The last several days, all British establishments within and outside the towering walls of the Red Fort, from armored *kotwalis* to family-bungalows – all had been sensing an inexplicable and unprecedented tension of impending violence. It is only during such times that precede exceptional and monstrous viciousness that even the unpainted walls, the quaking windows, creaking staircases and gawking doors of both palaces and poor dwellings begin to breathe with unexplained terror. Humans are unable to smell the reek of future blood... but these seemingly lifeless structures, built and destroyed in unison with the fortune of the ground where they stand, never fail to intuit an approaching catastrophe.

But that the genocide would unfold with such brutal rapidity was something that neither the living nor the unliving had envisaged.

On this hot summer day of May 1857, the sixteenth day of the holy month of Ramzaan, in the few hours between dawn and dusk, every inch of the muddy streets of Delhi was soon to be sprinkled with British blood.

Not all of the Englishmen had first responded with immediate and urgent measures. While some of them did raise somewhat of an alarm within their own official working groups and households in the hours leading to the full-blown sepoy assault, none of them could foresee the imminent catastrophe that was riding towards Delhi from Meerut with a tornado of dust.

That morning, still living under the illusion that the East India Company was in full and absolute control, the strapping young Robert D'Cruze had planned to take decisive action. Supremely confident of the loyalty of his force of cavalry and infantry, he had decided to unleash a terrorizing flag-march – a demonstration of the brute blade-muscle and fire-power of his Regiment across all the sensitive neighborhoods of Delhi. With Mastaan on his side, Robert felt almost intoxicated with power at most times. Even in the Bandookbaaz's physical absence, his confidence was undeterred. He sent for his troops even as he awaited the British Resident's approval.

Neither came.

The application seeking permission for the flag-march never did reach the Resident Simon Fraser. The messenger was hacked to pieces on the way.

And none of Robert's sepoys showed up for duty despite clear orders.

It was not long before Robert understood the reality of the day. As the news of British officers having been slaughtered by the mutineers from Meerut began to trickle in, and as English bungalows went up in screaming flames, the young Lieutenant was forced to accept the circumstances as they were. Left alone by his household staff and bereft of any comrade from the D'Cruze Regiment, Robert had readied all his weapons. He was not afraid for his own life. That was something he had thrown into the pitch and toss of military life every now and then. It was Fay. His little sister Fay. And the young Patricia. It was the safety of these two young girls that the Lieutenant was worried about.

Robert had fought and defeated the most daunting of adversaries. He was not one to back down now against the men he had trained himself. Against the men he loved. And yet, he knew their combat prowess well. He was not afraid of the Meerut cavalry or of the scoundrels from that day's prison-breaks. From a tactical vantage point he would pick them one by one with his new Enfield and old Brown Bess rifles – inflicting so many casualties that they would have no choice but to leave him and his family alone.

What he was truly bracing himself for was the frightening possibility of taking on his own sepoys – the formidable fighters of the D'Cruze Regiment.

If *they* attacked him, he knew he would not last more than a few shots.

And then suddenly, the arrival of one long-haired, almond-eyed warrior had shifted all the calculations and equations in Robert's favor.

Mastaan always tilted the scales.

Just by himself.

'They will not remain five hundred for long, Leftinant saahab. You take your position on the first-floor balcony and fire at the mob as it approaches us through the compound gates. Take Fay and Patricia with you. Quickly coach them on how to load a rifle, so you can keep firing without stopping. I will be on the ground floor. I will not let anyone set foot into the premises.'

Robert nodded. He knew he would be stronger from a high window sniper position. And he had no doubt in his mind that given the terrifying speed and accuracy with which Mastaan loaded and fired his guns, he would wreak havoc on the ground.

'Alright, Mastaan. It is you and me then,' said Robert, as he began to lead Fay and Pat up the first few steps of the wooden staircase.

'Do not worry, janaab. Chhagan and Shahbaaz will be here soon. We will be okay.'

Mastaan wanted to rush forward and take Fay in his arms. She looked so vulnerable, so lost... so scared. He wanted to tell her that everything will be okay. That he was there – standing firmly like a wall between her and any harm. That he loved her. That they would have a happy home one day. That they were destined to...

'I love him...'

The small group went silent.

'I love him, Robert... I love Mastaan.'

Fay was breathing nervously as she said those words aloud, looking into Mastaan's eyes, her voice breaking. She did not look at Robert. Whether he approved of her choice did not matter. Not anymore. Not when they appeared to be one bullet or one crude bomb away from the claws of death.

Robert, Mastaan and Pat stood gaping at Fay. Robert did not know how to deal with this new complicated detail under the trying circumstances that surrounded them.

Mastaan felt the immortal love of a thousand lives showered on him in this one moment.

The seventh city of Delhi was once again weaving its cruel magic. Just as the air was rendered thick with the curdling lust for blood, it was sowing the tender seeds of everlasting love.

It was Delhi's way of cocking a snook at the writers of its cosmic destiny.

It was the eternal city telling the ruthless Gods...

You can scorch me to ashes over and over again.

But every single time, I shall rise.

Every single time...

...it is love that shall prevail.

Gaddaar!

Married Officers' Quarters, near Metcalfe House, 0730 hours, 11th May 1857

Babban walked in front of the riotous mob, wearing a *topi*, white *kurta* and a green checkered *lungi*. Looking every bit like the street-fighter that he was, his banyan-like girth stood out amidst all the others walking behind him. The notorious local gangster brandished a thick bamboo *lathi* resting on his shoulder, the weapon's tip banded with a metal ring. The flattened ring was stained with fresh and mostly innocent blood of British women and children smashed to death in their sleep or when on their knees, begging for mercy, for a trace of compassion.

The mob's next stop was the D'Cruze residence. Not only was it in their destructive circuit, it also housed, as told to Babban by a disgruntled ex-servant of the household, two beautiful firangi girls. One of them, as per the villain's account, was 'made of milk, honey and rose'.

The scoundrel spoke of Fay.

The gigantic gangster and his henchmen, all marching under the garb of freedom fighters, maligning the name of the true Tilangas from Meerut, advanced towards the D'Cruze bungalow. The vile Babban's mouth was now watering at the thought of the two white girls at his absolute mercy.

What he did not know was that there was a mountain standing in the way.

Unlike what Robert had expected, Mastaan was nowhere near or behind any cover. He sat on the entrance stairs of the house, in direct line of sight from the entry gate twenty meters away. Two loaded rifles were by his side and two armed muskets were dug into his belt at the back. An unsheathed, gleaming *talvaar* stood in front of him, his arms resting on the sword's handle. This was Mastaan's favorite battle stance, resembling that of a panther crouching before a murderous leap.

As a yelling miscreant kicked the gate open and scores of men began stumbling into the compound in the hope of making another killing, this time their greed for gold whetted with the lust for soft white flesh, a chilling shot rang out. In the next moment, the escaped convict who had broken open the gate lay dead, a generous surge of blood oozing from his viciously fractured forehead.

Robert D'Cruze's rifle had found its first mark.

Another moment of deathly silence was followed by a chilling roar. Hundreds of attackers yelled in unison, none willing to walk a step further.

The Lieutenant turned momentarily and smiled at the two petrified girls who were crouching next to him and trying their best to stuff pellet and gunpowder into his heavy rifles.

'These are not my Hindustani soldiers, ladies. These cowards are petty criminals!' he exclaimed, almost jubilantly.

In the next second, he once again took aim and was ready to open fire.

Mastaan now stepped forward.

He walked slowly towards the bloodthirsty crowd at the gate, one rifle dangling on his left shoulder while the other was in an attack-ready grip in his right hand, finger on trigger. Within a moment the horde of hooligans went abuzz with the murmur of a name.

'Mastaan...'

'Mastaan...'

'Bandookbaaz...!'

Almost all of them knew of him. Those who did not, knew him now.

'Leave now if you hold your life dear!' announced Mastaan, staring into the collective eyes of the rabid mob like an angry lion looks onto a pack of hungry dogs.

It was now that Babban presented himself at the front of the crowd, albeit very cautiously. He had no intent to lock horns directly with the great Mastaan himself.

'Gaddaar!' he screamed, pointing at the formidable fighter standing between him and his loot. 'Traitor!'

Mastaan was unfazed at the cheap rhetoric. As far as he was concerned, the crowd of cowards facing him was the real traitor. Those men betrayed the Hindustani values of fairness in battle, of respect for women and protection of children, and of valor and honor in war.

The mob is a gullible collective. Within moments the entire gathering of attackers discovered a newfound justification for their shared animosity against the Bandookbaaz. Emboldened by their numbers, they started to inch forward, all of them now chanting the convenient slogan –

'Gaddaar!'

'Gaddaar!'

'Gaddaar!'

Mastaan was now contemplating his next course of action. He did not want to kill his own countrymen, even if they were rapists and murderers. He was mentally planning his moves to non-fatally incapacitate the first wave of rioters that was heading towards him.

Something happened suddenly just then and the large head of the cruel Babban seemed to turn momentarily disbalanced on his shoulders... before leaving his headless body and tumbling to the ground.

A white horse had appeared from nowhere, leaping over the fence of the bungalow and riding past the mob like a hurricane.

It was Shahbaaz, Mastaan's friend and protégé from the D'Cruze Regiment.

With a single sweep of his heavy talvaar, he had sliced Babban's head clean from his shoulders.

No questions asked.

No debates entertained.

Anyone charging towards Mastaan was a natural enemy for the entire D'Cruze Regiment.

They were a pack of wolves.

The long-bearded, arrogant and indescribably valiant Shahbaaz turned to look at Mastaan and quipped. He could never let go of a chance to crack a joke, however ill-timed it happened to be.

'Too much talk for one day, wasn't that, O glorious Bandookbaaz?!'

Mastaan rolled up his tense eyes, smiling a tired yet relieved grin at Shahbaaz, who looked suitably dramatic atop his fine snowy steed.

Shahbaz's dramatic entry caused the gang of men who had come thinking they would violate young girls and murder innocents scoot like a nest of mice. Shahbaaz then dismounted and walked towards his heroic mentor.

'Mastaan dada... what are we to do?' he asked, now in a state of daze and confusion

The momentary humor was all gone. Mastaan did not understand exactly what Shahbaaz wanted to know.

'We cannot keep Robert saahab and the girls in this bungalow, Shahbaaz. It will be attacked again sooner or later. There is only one place they would be safe. And that is at Chhagan's house in Churi Walan. Our sister Sujata will keep Fay and Pat hidden in her secure company, till reinforcements arrive from other garrisons.'

Shahbaaz did not respond for a few seconds. And then he spoke with great dejection, shaking his head.

'Mastaan dada... Chhagan is killing every white man he can find. He is burning English homes, torching churches and capturing cannons.

A madness seems to have come over him in the last hour or so. He is behaving like a bloodthirsty monster, dada. Just minutes ago, he hacked Padre Jennings with his own sword, in the very home of the unfortunate priest.

He has lost his mind, Mastaan. He is not the Chhagan Dubey we have known.'

The Armies of Timur

Delhi, 0800 hours, 11th May 1857

The Badshah felt as if he was a thirty-year old prince once again, with enough energy and vitality running through his veins for him to ride war-horses, take a dozen concubines and go for his favorite game-hunts.

After decades he had drawn his sword and was pacing around his courtyard overlooking the Jumna clasping it in his suddenly strong hands.

Without a single military or political move from his side, Bahadur Shah Zafar had suddenly emerged as the chosen Emperor for entire Hindustan. When he went to bed an old, haggard, puppet of a King on the night of the 10th of May, he could never have imagined that he would wake up the next morning to be in command of vast, highly-skilled and trained legions of infantry and cavalry. Overnight, like he was living a spectacular dream, Zafar had transformed from a feeble figurehead to a mighty monarch.

It was as if there was some magical, otherworldly force unleashing an all-powerful spell in favor of the old king, rewriting his destiny.

The dark powers of the half-faced conjurer were tampering with the forewritten pages of karma... and distorting them.

And once again, in his hour of unexpected and unfathomable glory... Zafar once again chose to blur out the price he had promised in return.

The rebels from Meerut had crossed the Bridge of Boats and ridden straight to the royal palace. They had demanded an immediate audience with the King himself. When after initial reservations and anxieties Zafar did present himself, they offered their unquestioned service and allegiance to him, and pronounced him to be the Emperor of all of Hindustan once again.

The choice of the freedom army was logical and strategic. They knew that if they were going to take on the full force of the remaining British military, they would need to unite all the native troops and commanders of the East India Company. And not just them. Support would be needed from the hundreds of princely states that dotted the Company's Hindustani empire. This was not going to be an easy task given the diversity of religions, castes, regional politics and the enormous egos of the Rajas and the Nawabs. Bahadur Shah was, therefore, the most acceptable and the most uncontroversial choice - under whose banner the entire revolution or struggle for independence could be rallied.

Vacillating as always, Zafar had at first rejected the sepoys' offer. He was not able to believe that a formidable military had just arrived at his doorstep and were willing to accept his kingship just like that. He suspected some serious foul play. Why would these men, who were capable of defeating the greatest armies in the field of battle, submit to his senile persona, his empty coffers and his non-existent army? But as the hours ticked by and a larger number of sepoy commanders began to bow in front of his silver throne, the reality slowly began to sink in.

In no time, the intoxication of brute military power began to slowly percolate into the royal consciousness. In a matter of two hours Bahadur Shah had journeyed from being a hapless pensioner to being perhaps the most powerful ruler in the entire Asian sub-continent!

One man was not at all at ease with the turn of events.

As Ahsanullah walked into the sunlit courtyard and saw the Emperor in an annoyingly triumphant mood, his fear turned into anger.

'Bend your knees in worship, jahanpanaah,' advised a trembling Ahsanullah. 'Seek the forgiveness of almighty Allah. Only He can deliver you from this dark magic. This cannot... will not end well for anyone, my King!'

The Emperor's physician and trusted friend had wasted no time in reminding the Badshah that whether it was the abrupt and fearless shot fired by Mangal Pandey, the swift victory of the Meerut mutineers or the sudden descent of a fantastical army at his regal feet – it was perhaps all the doing of the half-faced dervish from the black cavern situated right below where they sat now.

But when blood-spells are unleashed by warped and accomplished sorcerers who dwell partly in the realm of the dead, the first territory they conquer is the mind of their unsuspecting victim. Then... his soul. And finally... his bloodline!

In this case, it was the poor old Zafar who was the unfortunate victim.

Even as he rejoiced at what he thought was the revival of his dynasty on the throne of Hindustan, even as he imagined himself perched on a rebuilt *Takht-e-Taoos* or the Peacock Throne, even as his wild musings took him to the battlefields of Afghanistan, Deccan, Java and Sumatra with his forces routing the enemy and reacquiring the empire that his ancestor Aurangzeb once ruled, he was least bothered about his pact with the half-faced black-magician in that grotesque river-cave.

His physician, on the other hand, was worried. Zafar had struck an unspeakable bargain with the dangerous wizard and was behaving insanely in pretending to have forgotten all about it. Or was he not pretending? Either way, Ahsanullah was exceedingly nervous.

'*Aalampanaah*, today you have an army larger than even that of Timur Lang himself! Out of nowhere! But do you remember what you traded this against, my lord?'

The Mughal monarch kept up his melodramatic prancing, attempting to swing his heavy sword in the air, barely able to get it a foot above the marble floor.

'Who do you think I should appoint as the Governor of the royal treasury once it starts to overflow with gold, rubies and diamonds, Ahsanullah? These... these... lunatic but valiant young men are bound to flood the royal coffers with riches!'

The palace physician could not believe his ears.

The old fool has finally lost his mind.

Ahsanullah once again repeated his question, injecting more urgency and alarm into his voice.

'Badshah, what did you promise the evil dervish in return for armies larger than those of Timur Lang? Do you remember, jahanpanaah?!'

'I PROMISED HIM NOTHING... !!'

Ahsanullah was taken aback at the sudden and fierce reaction from Zafar. He stood at a distance, looking away from the direction in which his friend and doctor stood.

Slowly, the possessed Emperor turned.

Once again, his eyes were completely black. His head was twisted to one side. Zafar did not reside in that body. It was someone else.

Or so the trembling physician imagined.

This time the accent with which the old King's contorted body spoke sounded like the words of a young, arrogant... dead Britisher.

'I did not promise *him* anything that I am not willing to give!' screamed the horror of a voice from the twisted mouth of Zafar.

'Let the firangi take them away...!

Let them take all *three* of them away!!'

It was now that Ahsanullah's nerve gave way. He could immediately tell that he was not speaking to Bahadur Shah Zafar anymore. What kind of a lost, perverted and lustful creature could forget what Zafar was willfully renouncing?

As the royal physician bowed and took rushed leave of his King, he could hear the entire palace reverberate with a mad echoing laughter...

...the horrifying cackle of the half-faced dervish!

The One-Eyed Horseman

Delhi, 0900 hours, 11th May 1857

They slipped from one narrow back-lane of the walled city into another. Mastaan was leading the group.

By now the whole city of Delhi had erupted in violent chaos. Within a couple of hours of the Tilangas riding into the gates of the Laal Qila, the entire populace was in a grip of rampage and terror.

With their own demonstration of pillage and killing, the Meerut soldiers had instilled even the Delhi troops of the Company with passionate hatred against all British and Europeans. British families were being dragged out of their homes and hacked to death in full public glare. In that hour of vicious madness, the mutineers made a horrible mistake. A mistake they would pay for with not only rivers of their own blood but also that of thousands of ordinary residents of Delhi. Consumed by hate and mob frenzy, they began to murder not just the soldiers and officers of the Company Bahadur, but also their women and children.

And it was this one dishonorable act that would forever take away the unblemished magnificence of a great revolution from these men. History would write about the spectacular uprising of 1857 over and over again, it would hail the sacrifices made by these fearless warriors, and yet shy away from unquestioningly bestowing the immortal glory of freedom fighters upon these valiant yet momentarily misdirected troops.

With white men, women and children being put to the sword on every street and every corner of the wailing city, Mastaan and Shahbaaz knew they had to keep Robert, Fay and Pat away from the murderous mobs. Covered from head to toe in *burkhas* picked up from the orderly billets of Robert's bungalow, Fay and Pat looked like regular womenfolk of the Muslim quarters. Robert too had been disguised, as best as his white skin permitted, in native clothes.

However, they all knew time was running out. It would not be long before they are discovered and furiously attacked.

'We need to get off these lanes, Mastaan. How far did you say Ballimaran was?' enquired Robert in a hushed tone, as they hurriedly moved from one back alley to another.

With Chhagan's parental home not being an option anymore, Mastaan had only one place in the whole city where he was sure Fay and the others would be safe. The house of Mirza Ghalib was still far, but it was the only refuge the Bandookbaaz could think of. The news of his Chhagnu murdering unarmed men had stabbed him in the core of his heart. He decided that as soon as he had made sure that the D'Cruze household was safely settled at the famous Nausha Mian's residence, he would set out to find Chhagnu. Chhagnu had to be stopped. This insanity had to be stopped.

'Another half hour's walk, janaab,' replied Mastaan.

'Are you sure Mirza Ghalib will offer us shelter? Emotions are running high, Mastaan. How are we so sure he would not direct the mobs to us on the sly?' Robert probed. Given the mayhem all around and the inhuman butchering of British families, his concern was understandable. Mirza Ghalib was, at least from appearances, a Muslim nobleman of the Mughal court.

'Do not worry, Leftinant saahab, I know Mirza Nausha well. He is a human being first before being anything else.'

With these words he exchanged a quick glance with Fay, whose beautiful blue eyes were a giveaway even from behind the hijab.

Mastaan's whole world was now centered around those innocent, beatific eyes.

As the five of them hurried along in the maze of Delhi's tightly packed residential neighborhoods, Mastaan's mind and concentration were unwavering. He was on a single-minded quest to get Fay to safety. He knew everything was changing. He was aware that very soon he would be hit by some extremely difficult choices that would need to be made – unity versus loyalty, religion versus humanity, brotherhood versus propriety. But the hardest of all choices was going to be what the Bandookbaaz of the D'Cruze Regiment was dreading the most.

It was going to be his fierce patriotism for Hindustan versus his eternal, intense, immeasurable love for Fay.

They did not expect their luck to run out so soon. As they turned around a corner into a narrow pathway amidst houses on both sides, a hysterical looking British rider came galloping straight towards them at a frenzied speed. Dressed in what looked like just his underclothes, he was swinging a service-issue sword ominously.

Clearly unaware that three of the five pedestrians facing him were English, the rider seemed ready to pounce on them with his gleaming scimitar.

Not prepared to take a human life unless it became absolutely necessary, Mastaan reacted with dazzling alacrity. Picking up and flinging a brick lying on the ground he struck the horseman straight in the face, sending the disbalanced rider flying into the drainage gutter.

Before the fallen Englishman could scramble up on to his feet, they had passed him by. But even in that split second, Mastaan noticed one peculiar detail.

Despite being in such a debilitated state, the young Englishman looked unapologetically conceited.

From what Mastaan could see, the incapacitated Britisher had only one eye. There was a pirate flap on the other.

What the Bandookbaaz did not know then...

...was that the two of them were fated to meet again.

Kashmiri Gate

Delhi, 0930 hours, 11th May 1857

They slaughtered and waited.

The British Main Guardroom lay close inside the walls of the Laal Qila, only a few steps away from the Kashmiri Gate. After the general massacre of Europeans was out of the way on the streets of Civil Lines, Daryaganj, Chandni Chowk, the cantonment and the bazaars, the rebels had turned their attention to the British strongholds in the city.

Among the first few prominent Britishers to fall was the Resident himself. At the Calcutta Gate of the city, Simon Fraser had been cut to pieces in front of his own native troops as he had tried to flee following a gallant attempt to confront the mutineers. The next assassination was of the so-called priest Padre Jennings. And this was by no measure a shock to the citizens and rebels of Delhi. Much to the disquiet and heartburn of both Hindus and Muslims of the city, the zealot Jennings had carried out his conversion and proselytization activities with bitter disregard for the natives' religious sensitivities. As it turned out, he and his family paid a horrible price for this callousness.

And the lead executioner of this bloody mayhem was none other than a man who, till even a couple of hours ago, had firmly believed that the uprising against their British masters would have no violent implication for innocent civilians, women and children. A man who was committed to fighting all battles with honor, who had never once attacked an unarmed adversary and who had often risked his life to protect the destitute. The same man was now beheading and impaling European families with surgical meticulousness and fanatical hate.

Transformed from a righteous and brave warrior into a murdering monster almost abruptly, this man was none other than the Subedaar-Major of the D'Cruze Regiment.

The brutal rape of a young girl by two drunk British soldiers, and her eventual suicide the previous night, could not have come at a worse time. It was all happening as if a sinister ethereal power was scripting the chronicles of Dilli with crimson ink.

The entire city of citadels would weep oceans of blood, both white and brown, young and old, vile and pure - in order to atone for this horrendous depravity that had befallen its soil.

A city that fails to live up to its sacred duty of protecting its woman and offering her an unfettered life of freedom, liberty and free-will, does not remain anything more than a rotting graveyard in the eyes of the Gods. For the creators of heaven and earth, of the stars and the galaxies, such a city's dwellers become walking corpses and every speck of sand becomes cursed till eternity. One single woman violated embodies the tearing abuse of the Mother Goddess, of *Prithvi* herself, of all of Creation and of the cardinal principles of love, acceptance, procreation, civilization and most of all... humanity.

Delhi was going to pay a price that would lacerate it in blood and tears for generations.

When destiny's hand chooses to unleash carnage and destruction upon humankind, it finds an instrument to execute its cosmic will from among humankind itself.

The vicious abuse and death of poor innocent Sujata was the ghastly method fate had selected to transform the goodhearted Chhagnu into a cruel killer.

At this hour, for every British soul walking on the streets of Delhi...

...Chhagan Dubey was the Reaper's scythe.

The Main Guardroom near the Kashmiri Gate was now in control of the rebel army, led by Chhagan Dubey in this part of Delhi. The *ghadar* or rebellion had now spread to every corner of the burning city. European soldiers manning the Main Guard were quickly slaughtered. Chhagan Dubey now waited for the next batch of British troops to arrive from the cantonment barracks.

He waited for them, his sword dripping with fresh English death.

After about half hour, the British reinforcements appeared. And they were not alone. Along with the European regiments there were Indian troops from the 38th, 54th and 74th Infantry companies that were stationed in the Mughal capital. With this large contingent also lumbered along two devastating field guns.

The rebel soldiers stood no chance had this formidable force had chosen to attack them. But today was not a day when Chhagan Dubey was going to let anything come in the way of his vengeance. He rode forward with a loaded rifle in his hand till he came within the native army's earshot. Kashmiri Gate and the Main Guardroom were tactically critical for the success of the day. The Subedaar-Major decided to address his countrymen who stood facing him from the other side, imprisoned in British uniform tunics.

Not as much of a natural leader of men as his long-haired friend, Chhagan kept it simple. His words were reinforced by the splitting grief in his voice.

'This is not a mutiny, my brothers! This war is for liberty... yours, mine... this *bhoomi's*! The Company Bahadur has built its empire on the foundation of the dead bodies of our brothers and ancestors. Yet they treat us worse than slaves. Yesterday they violated my sister. Tomorrow they will rape yours! The time to pick sides has come, brothers! Fight and die for this imperial dragon. Or raise your sword for the glory of a free Hindustan!'

Dubey spoke from his enraged, mourning heart - and his words hit home.

Not one Indian trooper from the British side raised his gun when commanded to open fire on the rebel Subedaar-

Major. It was not long before the British soldiers and officers realized their precarious and vulnerable position. Loud, angry murmurs could now be heard from the three Hindustani companies of infantry.

It was at this time that Robert D'Cruze rode into the Kashmiri Gate. He had galloped like the wind to reach the Guardroom, after having left his sister and her friend in the comparative safety of a Ballimaran haveli. The two big field guns stood blocking the Kashmiri Gate, both cannons aimed towards the Subedaar-Major and his men. The place was already littered with mutilated corpses of several British officers and soldiers.

Impending violence was hanging heavy in the air.

Within minutes of Chhagan's impromptu address, the soldiers assembled behind the British officers had begun to break ranks and had walked towards the rebel army to join it. With even this last battery of troops defecting, British slaughter was now imminent.

It was a split moment before Chhagan prepared to fire the first shot towards the handful of English officers that a voice rang out.

'Subedaar-Major Chhagan Dubey! Stand back! What is the matter with you?!'

Robert D'Cruze now rode to the front of the anxious Company officers and placed himself right between the mutineers and their easy prey.

'What are you doing, Chhagan? What has come into you?' demanded Robert, unable to believe that his trusted, virtuous Subedaar-Major had transformed into this bloodthirsty messenger of death.

'Get out of the way, Leftinant saahab,' replied Dubey, unmoved by the presence of his once-loved regiment commander. 'You are the only Englishman who shall see today's sunset alive. Move over!'

Robert could see Chhagan's face now. It was a macabre version of the smiling Chhagnu the Lieutenant remembered. Dripping with hate and insanity, the Subedaar-Major's eyes were a giveaway. Within a few seconds Robert could tell that his Subedaar-Major was not there anymore. The man facing him was dead from within... seeking death all around him.

'Let these officers leave with me, Dubey...' Robert spoke cautiously, not letting his word or tone aggravate the bloodlust in Chhagan.

Chhagan broke into a sudden guffaw, turning to look at his fellow rebels, expressing his disbelief at the absurd proposition from Robert in cruel humor.

'They are all dead men, Robert saahab... save yourself while you can,' replied Dubey coldly after his untimely laughter had subsided as suddenly as it had erupted.

It was a stalemate.

Despite the unrelenting murderous instinct having consumed his soul in its entirety, the Subedaar-Major had a sliver of a heart still beating inside of him. His uncontrollable and violent aversion against all British notwithstanding, he was not going to harm his erstwhile friend and Lieutenant. They had bled for one another. They had saved each other's lives several times. He was not going to kill his D'Cruze saahab today.

And D'Cruze saahab was refusing to leave Kashmiri Gate unless he took all the remaining English officers and men with him.

'Look, Chhagan... you have killed the Resident already. You have slaughtered the Padre and his family. Hundreds of other Europeans have been hacked to pieces throughout the city. There has been enough bloodshed today. You know this chapter will not end here. You know the Company Bahadur will strike back with such devastating retribution that all of India will drown in blood. We both, you and I... we don't need to try and end it all today, end it all now. Let these men go, Chhagan. Let them go in the name of our friendship. Let them go for old times' sake, my brother.'

Chhagan was listening. The goodness of his heart was now in a fierce duel with the sorrowful hatred that his soul was burning with.

Before he could respond, Robert said something that meant everything to the Subedaar-Major.

'Even Mastaan is with me. He saved me. He saved Fay and Pat...'

'BECAUSE HE DOES NOT KNOW!' screamed back Chhagan, his voice hoarse with angst.

With this outburst, Chhagan Dubey broke into tears. His next words tore deep into the hearts of everyone present at the gate of Delhi that fateful morning.

'Mastaan does not know what your people did to my little Sujata!

He does not know what those two British beasts subjected *his* little sister Sujata to!

He is not even aware that she is gone!

Take your men and run, Robert! I shall leave this place now, for I do not want to stain my hands with your righteous blood. But my fellow freedom fighters are thirsting for vengeance. So, run away! Ask your men to jump off the fort bastions and flee. Hide where you can!

The minute Mastaan finds out the horrible truth about our little girl...

...he will drink every last drop of British blood!'

'God help the people of Delhi...'

Delhi, 1000 hours, 11th May 1857

'I have no words to thank you, Nausha Mian. I had nowhere else to go.'

'You don't have to thank me, Mastaan. In just one cursed morning, the air of this city has turned from the breeze of jannat to the raging fire of hell. This is the least any human being can do for another when Allah has chosen to punish us all alike.'

After two hours of hiding and running in the tightly packed neighborhoods of Delhi, avoiding screaming mobs and murdering parties, Mastaan, Fay and Patricia had somehow managed to reach the doorstep of Mirza Ghalib in mohalla Ballimaran.

Despite desperate insistence from both Mastaan and Fay, Robert had decided to break away from the group and try to meet his fellow officers at the Main Guardroom – the only martial stronghold he hoped to find still in British control.

After the departure of Robert, Mastaan had asked Shahbaaz to ride out as well for a recce. He wanted Shahbaaz to find out what exactly was going on in the city. More importantly, Mastaan had requested his regiment-mate to seek out Chhagan.

The young Bandookbaaz of the D'Cruze Regiment was now simply following his heart, minute by minute, hour by hour. The war he had dreaded for so long had finally erupted. He knew he had his countrymen on one side. His loyalty for the East India Company was now openly pitted against his love for the motherland.

But could one night of bizarre events suddenly make his friend and superior Robert D'Cruze his enemy? Chhagan was right all the way, this Mastaan had slowly come to believe. Even Bakht Khan was not wrong when he spoke of the reality of the East India Company. But was all that enough to make Mastaan kill every white man he encountered today and forever? Till a few hours ago they were parading in step with British officers. Now was he to slaughter them, one and all, in cold blood?

The one thing he was sure of was that his sword and his guns would not... could not remain neutral through this dark hour.

The one thing he was convinced about was that the safety of Fay lay above everything else. Outside of his day-dreams and his romantic fantasies, they had not been married or engaged. Nor was their love commonplace enough to be accepted by the complex society they lived in. While they had kissed a few times, they never made love. And yet, she was everything for Mastaan.

Everything.

After they had had a wash and a few minutes' rest, Mirza Ghalib's wife, Umrao Begum, served her tired guests a simple meal of kebabs, roti and lamb soup. These were from the leftovers of the *sehri* or pre-dawn meal they had eaten in the household that day of Ramzaan. Ghalib being a non-conformist by every measure, joined his guests for the repast.

It was the illustrious shaayar who spoke first, as they began to break bread together.

'How can we blame the Tilangas when it is actually the people of Dilli that have turned on their fellow residents, Mastaan? It is not the rebel soldiers but the inhabitants of the Khanam Bazaar that are leading the looting and the massacre. The criminals of the city have joined the ranks of the rebels and so have some miscreant wrestlers, butchers and paper-makers from the Kaagazi Galli. The kotwali has been ransacked. The scoundrels even attacked the bank and killed the Beresford family – women and children included. The streets of Dariba at Chandni Chowk are flowing with blood and there is rioting and plundering all around. Ya Allah! What fate have you sent our way? What do you have in mind for my beloved city?' lamented Ghalib, unable to swallow even a morsel of the kebab and roti in his plate.

'Please calm down, Mirza Nausha,' said Mastaan, his hand on the bent knee of the old poet. 'I am sure things will come back to normal soon.'

Ghalib smiled feebly and shook his head.

'No, they won't, Bandookbaaz... no, they won't. Like I told you before, the greatest shaayar Meer was destined to witness the burning of Dilli before embarking upon his journey to the afterlife. And Asadullah Baig is fated to see the demise of this golden city before he shuts his eyes forever.'

They all sat listening to the great poet, as he continued to pour out his heart.

'*Mian*, they are not even sparing people taking refuge in churches, temples and mosques. And it is the Dilli-waalahs who are pointing out the hiding places of Christian families, rejoicing as the criminals and some Tilangas hack them down. What kind of men are these, Mastaan? Were we not better off under the Company rule till a few hours ago? Will these men, who fill their carts, camels and pockets with jewels and gold coins tainted with the blood of innocents, be the next masters of Dilli and Hindustan?'

The room went silent. What Mirza Ghalib had just said was the question haunting all of them. While Mastaan had tried to console the crestfallen shaayar, he could tell that this nightmare was not going to end anytime soon. The native army had taken up arms against their British masters and, as it had been made amply clear in all the words and actions of the East India Company in the past decades, this meant a war to the very end.

The Company would not stop till it had shot or hanged every single mutineer. And the freedom army was not going to rest till the Europeans were summarily thrown out of Hindustan to the last man.

It was going to be a fight till either side had even a single bullet left unfired.

'You are right, Mirza. I am as stunned to see the mindless violence perpetrated by my city's inhabitants and even some of my comrades as you are. In the heat of the moment they have clearly lost their path. This was not the pious and patriotic struggle that they have been discussing and drawing plans for over months. The killing of English women and children is going to be an unpardonable blot on the character of this uprising.'

Mastaan took a spoonful from his soup bowl and continued.

'But I know one thing for sure, Mirza – these sipahis are thorough patriots and each one of them is willing to give up his life for the dream of a unified Hindustan, free from foreign yolk. Do you think they are not aware that a monstrous British military will soon lumber towards them? Do you think they don't know that most of them will not live to see the other side of this war? But they are still here, Mirza, still ready to battle... till their last breath.'

'That does not matter, Mastaan!' snapped Ghalib. 'One man's patriot is another man's monster! Nothing justifies the murder of hapless Christian families, surrounded and slaughtered by five hundred armed men!'

'You are absolutely right again, Mirza Nausha. But I have seen mobs before. These men are trained in the art of war for sure, but do not forget that at the end of the day they are simple, poor, illiterate men who had no malice in their hearts when they chose to get conscripted with the Company Bahadur. They are only avenging what they have seen the British do over more than a century to their own villages, homes and families. The ruthless reign of the English, the rendering of millions of craftsmen, weavers and spinners penniless, the impoverishment of farmers and peasants all over Hindustan, the frequent famines, the crippling of Indian merchants and their workers, the killing of Rajas and their ill-equipped armies without any provocation, the usurping of kingdoms, the mindless undermining of people's faiths... what all do you want me to highlight?'

Mastaan's voice had reached a high pitch by now. He had everyone's rapt attention, including that of his gracious host.

'Mirza, there was an entire family dying of starvation and disease behind each such peasant, each such weaver and each such soldier. My paltan and I fought for the Company relentlessly, but each day our conscience was tested. Chhagan is not wrong in what he says. Moreover, I do hang my head in shame as I hear the screams of a dying British family, but do you think the miscreants of Delhi or of the rebel army are the last to unleash such terror? Do you think such mob frenzies will never happen in a free Hindustan? When a bloody revolution begins, no one can control its cataclysmic flames. The British sowed the seeds of violence, Mirza. They are only reaping the gory harvest now. And this will not be the end, I know...'

The Bandookbaaz went silent, looking grimly at the floor, lost in evident worry.

'What do you mean, Mastaan?' asked Fay softly, keeping her empty bowl of lamb soup away.

Mastaan turned to Fay and Pat, and then slowly towards Mirza Ghalib and his begum. He knew about the gigantic war machinery and the cold brutality of the Company very well.

He spoke matter-of-factly.

'When the British return with their mammoth artilleries, their colossal garrisons and their most savage officers...

...God help the people of Delhi.'

The Tiger's Lair

Seringapatam, 4th May 1799

'I will first blow your head, *Sher*... and then I will steal all your gold!'

These were the words whispered into the ears of the Tiger of Mysore, as he writhed in pain and slashed his mighty sword even in the agonizing delirium of his final moments. Within the next few seconds, the greed-filled John McGowen had shot Tipu from behind his own senior officer's shoulder.

'What is the matter with you, McGowen?! We could have taken him alive...!' screamed Colonel Doherty, one of the senior commanders of the largest siege force to have ever marched on the face of the earth.

Son of Haider Ali, the dreaded battle commander and the de facto ruler of the kingdom of Mysore, Sultan Fateh Ali Saahab Tipu, better known as Tipu Sultan, rose to unparalleled military supremacy during his years of reign. Forever to remain a controversial and complex historical character when it came to his religious policies, Tipu was the last thorn in the way of the ambitious design of the East India Company to become the undisputed overlord of entire Hindustan. Tipu was a towering monarch, a winner of wars and a man who earned his name by killing a tiger singlehandedly during his teenage years. A military genius far ahead of his time, he was a personal friend of none other than the great Napoleon Bonaparte himself.

This was the fourth Anglo-Mysore war. And the final one at that. The East India Company had left nothing to chance this time. The behemoth of an army that took months to reach the moats of the Seringapatam Fort comprised not just British forces but also those of the Marathas and the Nizam of Hyderabad. This was an army so large that it was going to be a swift victory for the attackers. Or so everyone believed. The winning prize was not just the absolute domination of southern India, but also the greatest treasure in the world.

It was spoken in whispers across all of Hindustan, from the exclusive evening clubs of ambitious Company Generals to the mud huts of fantasy-struck peasants, that the Tiger of Mysore was the master of the earth's most priceless fortune - and that uncountable wealth lay buried somewhere, hidden in the underground crypts of the mysterious Seringapatam Fort.

What the invading military and its commanders did not know was that one British officer and his influential Indian friend from Delhi were a step ahead of everyone. John McGowen and Muntasir Bakhsh had hatched a cruel plot – first, to win over one of Tipu's most trusted confidantes with the lure of unimaginable wealth; and ending the traitor's life swiftly after he had directed them to the fabled treasure.

And second, to kill the Tiger of Mysore at any cost before he was captured.

The treasure had to be theirs...

...and theirs alone.

The reason behind this day's mad rage and vengeful frenzy of the British, Maratha and Nizam's armies was the determined and crushing resistance Tipu and his forces had put up. Not only had they withstood the siege for much longer than the aggressors had planned for, Tipu's forces had inflicted heavy casualties and damages on the blockading troops. Tactical night-attacks with camel-mounted Mysorean iron-boxed rockets had wreaked havoc in the invading army.

Finally, it was only after a turncoat betrayed his valiant king that the walls of Seringapatam were breached. The aggressors made their way into the fortress with hateful vehemence.

Leading the final stand of his remaining troops was the Sher-e-Mysoor himself – fighting with grit, ferocity and valor that the British had never witnessed before. Tipu was using rifles, muskets, swords and daggers... any weapon that he could find, eventually taking on twenty attackers all by himself.

John McGowen was watching every move of Tipu from a distance. By now they had the coveted map, Muntasir and he. The man who had betrayed his own king lay dead among the heaps of corpses, his throat slit cleanly by Muntasir Bakhsh from behind.

Muntasir had done his end of the job. It was now McGowen's turn to take care of his side of the plan. No doubt it was the harder of the two. The Englishman had to achieve what four full-scale wars of the Company had failed in doing.

He had to slay Tipu Sultan.

His sword struck the shields, armors and blades of the surrounding enemies with the crash of thunder. Sher-e-Mysoor was demonstrating why he was called so – Sher! Like the king of the jungle surrounded by a pack of hyena, Tipu fought on with spine-chilling desperation.

Despite his capital and his fort being overrun by enemy troops, unmindful of all his leading generals and commanders lying dead, unconcerned with the insurmountable odds against him – Tipu Sultan was refusing to give in. Drenched in his own blood, tired to the bone and wheezing for the want of breath, he went on... slashing, swinging, tearing and mauling any British or Maratha soldier that came within his hitting range.

Those who stood witness to this historical battle of one man against an entire army, would never forget the gleaming sword of Tipu Sultan.

McGowen could see that his superiors wanted to take Tipu prisoner. They were slowly closing in around him and none of them were firing a musket shot, something that would have ended the struggle swiftly. McGowen could not have allowed them to take the Tiger alive, because that would mean the treasure falling into the hands of the Company sooner than later. Even Tipu could not have withstood the torture of his women and children.

He had to act fast. Act now!

Loading a musket and drawing his scimitar, McGowen approached the site of the Sultan's final resistance, pretending to be fighting among the sincere soldiers who were braving the Tiger's onslaught. As he moved in, his eyes were dazzled by the purse that Tipu had tied to his waist. Greedy as a wolf, the young Britisher could not ignore the monarch's personal gem pouch. If Tipu was the master of the world's most famous treasure, what kind of select jewels would he keep close to his own person? McGowen now had a third goal.

Kill Tipu.

Snatch his purse.

Loot his treasure.

Never forgets.
Never forgives.

Delhi, 1100 hours, 11th May 1857

They were now lodged in the *barsaati* or the monsoon-chamber of the Ghalib household.

Even the Indian residents of Delhi who were found providing shelter to Europeans were being slaughtered. Informants, who pointed out houses where white men and women were hiding, earned suitable rewards. Those houses of course, along with their dwellers, were being burnt to ashes in no time.

In such a scenario, the risk being taken by Mirza Asadullah's family in offering a safe haven to Fay and Pat was nothing less than divine intervention for the girls on the run... and a shining example of compassion and humanity. Till now, Mastaan had believed that Ghalib was a fearless artist.

It was only today that he realized... Mirza Nausha was a fearless man in his very way of life.

When have the fearful ever become immortal?

Pat's nerves had somewhat calmed down after spending a couple of hours at the old, small yet impeccably maintained Ballimaran haveli. She found some reprieve in sleep.

Mastaan and Fay sat next to each other, both exhausted from the eventful morning's never-ending anxiety. The barsaati had two simple wooden beds. One was being occupied by the sweet Pat, while the other doubled up as a backrest for the young couple in love, sitting on the floor, shoulders rubbing. The room's walls were almost entirely made up of two-tiered barred windows, that permitted some breeze to flow in even on this sweltering hot morning.

Ballimaran was still some distance away from the rotting air of the burning Delhi neighborhoods, putrefied with the stench of scorching human flesh.

'You're alright, Fay?' asked Mastaan, after they had spent a few minutes in complete silence, just soaking in each other's much-needed touch and comforting presence.

'Yes,' she replied. 'And you?'

She slipped her fingers into his and clasped them tight as she snuggled closer to him.

'I am okay, Fay. Just don't know what is going on around us. How can a reasonably peaceful world turn into a mad slaughterhouse overnight? How can human beings, who have peaceably coexisted for years, suddenly turn into venomous foes, baying for each other's blood? I have fought scores of big and small battles. Bloodshed on the field of a military conflict is something we cannot wish away. Politics, conquest, wealth, power... all of those things are acceptable as they are.

The world cannot run without some men being ambitious and the others being at the mercy of these men.'

She was listening to him with deep and affectionate attention, as he continued to share his doubts and fears with her.

'But why should an innocent child be murdered? Why should a happy home be torched? And do you think this is going be as one-sided a massacre as it is appearing to be today? No, Fay. I have grown up within the precincts of the East India Company. The Company Bahadur never forgets. It never forgives. Today British blood is being spilled. The day is not far when Hindustani screams will rend through the air of Delhi. Our men are brave. But even in their vast numbers they are no match for the complex war-apparatus at the disposal of the Company.'

Fay was listening intently and thinking in parallel. She was angry at the marauders attacking homes and shops, and killing innocents in the name of religion, color and even patriotism. But more than that, she was stunned to see soldiers of the native army permitting the criminals of Delhi this cruel free run.

'But if these butchers are punished for their heinous deeds, would that not be fair justice, Mastaan? Why should these men be allowed to live after what they have done?'

Mastaan took Fay's hand in both his own and spoke with visible fondness.

'This is all not as simple as one would think, Fay. From the viewpoint of the British, the Company is probably not doing anything that it should not. After all, it is a merchant organization and should strive for profits in whatever manner it can. But when you come to the other side of the table, the Indian side, you will see a stark difference in the picture. No doubt some officers of the East India Company are righteous and fair, including your brother. But such people are nothing but a rare exception these days.'

Fay nodded. But her expression said that she did not really grasp what Mastaan was trying to say.

'Look, Fay... what has the Company not disrupted in this part of the world? Trade? Village economies? Industry? Land? Governance? Inheritance? Religion? Pride? They treat us nothing more than a country of barbarians. Every aspect of Hindustani life has been systematically uprooted and destroyed by the British. These men are not angry at their officers alone, Fay. They are not just a bunch of sipahis mutinying for better wages or superior working conditions. They are a manifestation of an entire sub-continent's rage. They truly are freedom fighters, my dearest.'

Fay looked unconvinced. She shifted in her place to partially face Mastaan and spoke candidly.

'To this I would say that it is all not so plainly black and white as you are making it out to be, Mastaan,' she protested, turning to look at her man in his eyes. She was not one to accept anything until her own intellect and instinct were in agreement.

'The East India Company has not been as much of a curse on India as you are describing. Okay, for a moment I agree that their methods of business have been coercive rather than cooperative. However, look at all the good the Company has done. The horrible practice of *Sati*, where a widow was expected to burn alive on her deceased husband's funeral pyre, has been abolished. Consider the Company's ironhanded onslaught on the centuries' old bane of *Thugee*. Widow remarriage and inheritance have been legalized only last year! Postal and telegraph services have been introduced, railways are being set up, canals are being constructed... can you not see all that, Mastaan?'

The Bandookbaaz of the D'Cruze Regiment was ready with many answers and debate points. He wanted to scream out to Fay that no amount of development or social reforms can ever justify the ruthless enslavement and exploitation of an entire sub-continent. But he held himself back and sighed. Deep in his heart he hoped that Fay and he would have a whole lifetime together to argue, to fight and to make up.

For now, he chose to remain quiet. This was a long debate and he did not want to engage in it with a tired and traumatized Fay, at least not at this time when every minute they had with each other was precious.

'I will go and find Chhagan, Fay. He seems to not be in his right senses. He needs me.'

'Yes, of course, Mastaan, please go. We are okay here,' said Fay, braving a smile. Just an inch below that forced smile she was petrified. On their way to Ballimaran they had witnessed a horrendous bloodbath on the streets, and like every European in Delhi that day, she was shaken to her soul.

Mastaan understood everything. Leaving Fay alone even for a minute at such a perilous time was the last thing he wanted to do. But he had to find Chhagan. Shahbaaz had also not come back till now. He had to know what was going on in the city. He had to find a way to get Fay and Pat away from the mayhem.

He nodded and smiled at the love of his life. He raised his hand and caressed her soft cheek with the back of his fingers.

'As soon as I am back, we need to get you and Pat out of Delhi. Things are only going to worsen in the city. You both have to escape before it is too late.'

'Whatever the case, I am not going anywhere without you, Bandookbaaz,' replied the blue-eyed English girl firmly.

Mastaan got up, changed his posture and turned to her, now sitting on his knees.

'You are not going anywhere without me, my love... in this life and all the others.'

Fay smiled again, this time for real. Her eyes were moist.

'In this life and all the others...' she repeated.

Mastaan bent forward and kissed her soft lips, followed by a long peck on her forehead.

As Mastaan equipped himself with his weapons and made his way to the barsaati's door, Fay called out to him softly.

'The girls in the service of Mrs. Ghalib told me about an unspeakable crime committed against an Indian girl last night, Mastaan. They say she was violated by two British soldiers, after which the poor soul killed herself by slitting her own throat with a knife. Do you know anything about this? Who was this girl?'

'I have no idea, Fay. May God bless her soul,' replied Mastaan, deeply perturbed at the news. 'It is a shame for our entire society that it is the victim of such abuse that inflicts further pain on herself, rather than the perpetrators of these monstrous crimes. Why should she be the one to pay for the sins of the fiends who assault her?'

Mastaan shook his head in dejection. 'Like I said, Fay, I do not know who the poor girl was.'

But the Bandookbaaz was not as distant from this painful episode as he thought.

He was going to discover the real horror behind it...

...just a flight of stairs away.

The Powder Magazine

Delhi, 1130 hours, 11th May 1857

Shahbaaz was waiting nervously for Mastaan in the courtyard of Mirza Ghalib's haveli. He had returned from the Kashmiri Gate after witnessing the dialogue between Chhagnu and Robert from a safe distance.

The young cavalryman was not sure how he was going to break the horrifying news to Mastaan.

The long-haired fighter of the D'Cruze Regiment climbed down the flight of stairs from the terrace of the house to where his friend was waiting. He was delighted to see Shahbaaz, but within a moment his happiness vanished. The expressions on both Shahbaaz and Mirza Nausha's faces were frighteningly disturbed.

'What is the matter, Shah?' enquired Mastaan, looking into the red eyes of his barrack-mate.

Shahbaaz just shook his head in extreme misery. They had all loved her. She had laughed with them as they had enjoyed meals cooked by her. She had tied a *raakhi* each year on the wrist of not just her real brother Chhagan, but also on those of Mastaan, Shahbaaz and Balram.

'Tell me, Shahbaaz... what is the matter??' Mastaan demanded, now grabbing hold of his friend's shoulders. His eyes were darting between those of Shahbaaz and Mirza Ghalib. 'Has something happened to Chhagnu...?'

It was the distraught shaayar who finally gathered the courage to break the heart-wrenching news. He walked up to Mastaan and looked at him with the tenderness that only wrinkled old eyes that have suffered unimaginable pain through their life-journey can muster.

'Your friend is alright, Mastaan. Or at least he is alive in the literal sense. But someone else has been lost, my dear...'

'Who, Mirza?' asked Mastaan. There was no one else he could think of. No one else meant anything much to him. Or so his confused mind erroneously concluded at that moment. Then why were Shahbaaz and Mirza Ghalib being so circumspect, so broken in their words? Was it Robert saahab who had been killed? Was it Balram?

Ghalib sat down on a *takhat* or wooden settee that was nearest to him. After a few moments of shaking his head in sorrowful dismay, he spoke the words.

'It is your friend's sister, Sujata, Mastaan. She was the girl who was wronged in the late hours of last night. Shahbaaz tells me what she meant for you all. It is for this reason your friend Chhagan has turned into a monster. He is only avenging his young sister, Mastaan... like any brother would do.'

As he heard these words from Ghalib, Mastaan's mouth went dry. He looked at Shahbaaz, then back at Ghalib. His head began to swirl, and his vision became dark. Drenched in cold sweat almost instantly, he started to stare around at the walls and corners of the haveli's courtyard. Not a moment more had passed before the legendary Bandookbaaz crashed to his knees, buried his face in his hands and wept uncontrollably... loud and gashed.

'No! No! No...!' he kept saying.

Mastaan's tears and his wounded cries now seemed to echo the dark bawling of the very city of Delhi.

'Meeting Chhagan at this time is of no use, Mastaan dada. He is in no frame of mind to listen to anyone... not even to you.'

After several minutes of mourning, Mastaan had somewhat calmed down. At least from the outside. He had splashed water on his face from a bucket and tied his long hair into a loose bun.

Shahbaaz was trying to dissuade him from any attempt to try and stop the slaughter that Chhagan was unleashing. What he did not know was that just like Chhagan, now even Mastaan was burning in the fire of hate. He did not know against whom that hate was directed. Shahbaaz had confirmed that the two debauch fiends who had committed this ghastly crime had already been chopped to pieces by Chhagan and his men. And yet, there was anger. Unbridled, irrepressible rage!

'Look dada, if Fay and Pat were not our responsibility, I would not have stopped you from anything. But at this time our first duty is to ensure their safety,' insisted Shahbaaz.

He was right. Shahbaaz had ridden through the city on his way to Ballimaran just minutes ago. From the disquieting updates he had provided about the state of Dilli and the lost British cause at the Kashmiri Gate, the violence was only becoming worse by the minute.

Mastaan wiped the remnants of his tears and tried to suppress Sujata's smiling face that had begun to haunt him every second now.

'Where is Chhagan at this time, Shah?'

At this enquiry Shahbaaz nodded briskly and sat next to Mastaan. It was as if this was the question he was waiting for.

'Mastaan dada, as we all can tell, there is going to be a major siege around Delhi. The Company's armies will be drawn from far and wide, right from the North Western part of the sub-continent to the Gurkha regiments in the East - and they will descend upon Delhi with all their might. The freedom army has declared its allegiance to Bahadur Shah, and it is being said that Indian troops from various British garrisons are going to converge in Delhi within the next few days, fortifying the city from inside the walls, fighting under a unified Mughal banner. They are saying that some of the Nawabs and Rajas will also be joining the ghadar with their armies.'

Mastaan sat still as a statue, staring at the broken floor of the courtyard. But Shahbaaz knew that the splendid fighter was listening to every word. He continued.

'As far as one can see, it is here that the decisive battle will be fought between the Indian freedom fighters and the East India Company. But dada, once larger rebel forces ride into

Delhi, it will be impossible for us to smuggle Fay and Pat out... not today, not ever. If a few thousand native soldiers have overrun the entire Mughal capital and have permitted the killing of nearly every Christian of the city within a matter of hours, imagine what a hundred thousand battle-hardened men will do.'

The Bandookbaaz was indeed listening to his friend carefully. In the frantic haste of escorting the two British girls to safety through a major part of that fateful morning, Mastaan had lost track of how the day was unfolding in the city. It was only now that he was able to grasp the gravity of the situation as well as the scale of the mutiny or of Hindustan's first war for independence.

'Dada... Chhagnu has killed Padre Jennings and his family. It was his men that cut the Resident Fraser down to pieces. Several other Europeans including Colonel Ripley have been butchered by his band of killers. But the worst is yet to come.'

'How so...?' asked Mastaan, wondering how much worse things could get from here.

He was being naïve. He had no idea what ghoulish, indescribable devastation lay in store in the coming days and weeks. The morning that had passed was not even a glimpse of the macabre nightmare that was inching towards Delhi.

Shahbaaz moved ahead with his quick and vital briefing.

'Leaving Balram and his men behind to kill the remaining British men at the Kashmiri Gate, our Subedaar-Major is now advancing towards a special target. If the rebel army captures this strategic asset, the British will *never* be able to quell the mutiny, and Delhi will be lost by them forever. While that may sound like a rejoicing fact for the freedom army and the Mughal Emperor, it will seal the fate of Fay and Pat... and perhaps yours and mine too.'

'What do you mean, Shah? Which strategic asset are you talking about?' asked Mastaan.

The situation had clearly escalated to a far more damaging scale than Mastaan had imagined. That violence and rioting abounded across the city was no secret. But that the rebel army would approach the old Zafar so speedily, that the Resident Simon Fraser would be killed within hours, that the Padre would be murdered in his own home and that Chhagan would organize a death-party so quickly, was all news to the Bandookbaaz.

'The gun-powder magazine, Mastaan dada. It will decide the fate of this war!' replied Shahbaaz in no uncertain terms.

His words hit Mastaan like a brick in the chest. It was within a second that the Bandookbaaz fully comprehended the ominous implications of what Shahbaaz was saying.

'How can that be, Shahbaaz? The magazine building is one of the most well-guarded structures in the city and it is under firm British control,' said Mastaan, in a desperate attempt to argue against the menacing reality they were faced with.

Shahbaaz replied patiently.

'As you know, dada, the powder magazine in Delhi is the largest stockpile of guns, ammunition, cannons and explosives across all British establishments in northern India. Apart from enormous quantities of field-gun and musket powder, it has almost an unlimited supply of cannon-grape, rifles, shells and bullets. If the rebel army captures this war-chest, the British will never be able to defeat them. With the powder-magazine supplying them with an inexhaustible cache of arms and ammunition, the rebel army will burn through all British blockades like child's play.'

Mastaan was quiet for a moment, before he concluded Shahbaaz's advice in simple words.

'So, basically, Shah, if Chhagan seizes control of the magazine, it is the end of the road for the East India Company?'

'Yes, dada...' replied Shahbaaz, unable to utter the other, more personal and more painful inference this had for Mastaan.

The Bandookbaaz did that for him without wasting any time.

'And if that happens, Fay and Pat will never leave Delhi alive.'

After a moment's pause, Mastaan completed his statement.

'Nor will I.'

The Flagstaff Tower

Delhi, 1215 hours, 11th May 1857

'You do realize what this will mean, Mastaan...?'

He did not respond, as he loaded his guns and ammunition pouches with shells.

'Mastaan, sweetheart... this amounts to you betraying your own people! Will you be able to live with that?' pleaded Fay.

Fay was totally unsure about what the Bandookbaaz had decided to do. He had come back up to the barsaati to tell her all about Sujata, about the morose killings of Fraser and Jennings, about the freedom army's propping up of the old Mughal Emperor... and to tell her about the pivotal role of the powder-magazine's precious arsenal in deciding which way this war was going to go.

But above all that, and to her absolute disbelief, he had told her that he was going to defend the magazine building for the British. If it had been lost already by the time he reached it, he would wrest it back from the rebels, no matter what that took.

As Shahbaaz had informed Mastaan, all gates of the city were now manned by rebel soldiers. All vehicles, carts and wagons were being checked thoroughly for any Europeans trying to escape. The unfortunate ones that were caught were being put to the sword immediately, no questions asked. The houses of both Hindu and Muslim nobles were being raided and searched in order to seek and murder any remaining Christians. It would not be long before the Ballimaran haveli was also attacked.

'Look at me, Mastaan... answer me!' demanded Fay yet again.

'What choice do I have, Fay?!' replied Mastaan sharply, irritable and helpless. 'The whole city is like a prison now. Thousands of men with bloodstained swords are looking for you and Pat! We cannot stay in this house for more than a few days or a couple of weeks at best without being discovered. If the East India Company lays siege around Delhi and loses – *we are all as good as dead, Fay.* And until I have even one drop of blood in my veins, I will protect you!

Let alone these men, even if I have to fight the Gods to keep you safe, I will!'

She held him in her arms, refusing to let him go.

It was time for Mastaan and Shahbaaz to leave. Mastaan had painted his face black and covered it with a dark scarf. Never one to wear his uniform with discipline anyway, he had discarded his buttoned-down red tunic in favor of a fitting leather armor that Shahbaaz had carried with him.

Shahbaaz also changed into civilian clothes and hid his face behind a white cotton veil. The two men knew they were going to come face to face with their own countrymen, perhaps with even their regiment-mates. Keeping their identities secret was going to be an important element of this mission if they did not want to declare an open war on their own friends.

'Think again, my Bandookbaaz. Think one last time. Is my life, Pat's life, your life... are any of these worth a lifetime of guilt that you are bound to carry within yourself after today, festering every day... reminding you of how you let down your people, your nation?'

Mastaan's forehead wrinkled and he closed his eyes, firming up the arduous decision in his mind, preparing himself for the aftermath of his deed today. When he opened his eyes after a few seconds, he appeared to be absolutely clear in his head.

'My love for my motherland is second to none, Fay. But you are all I have. All I have ever had! You give meaning to every breath I take. If I cannot be loyal to you, if I cannot protect you... what use will I be for my country or for my people? How can I be loyal to anyone or anything if I fail in my duty towards you? I have to do this, Fay. History may call me a villain, a gaddaar, a turncoat, a man blinded by love or whatever else it chooses to. But before I pay my country's debt, I have to pay my debt to you. Once I am done with that, my life will belong to the dust of Hindustan, Fay. But let me go today.'

Unmindful of Shahbaaz and Pat's presence in the room, Mastaan pulled Fay towards him and was about to kiss her when he remembered the still-fresh paint on his face.

'Oh sorry... I will not let my blackness stain your beautiful, fair face, Fay,' he said with a smile.

Mastaan was going to take all the blame, all the blemish, all the burden on his soul... and his soul alone.

She smiled back, but it was an extremely nervous one.

'Are you sure you can do this, Mastaan?' she whispered, trying not to look too scared.

The one virtue Mastaan was never short of was self-belief. He looked straight into her eyes and spoke matter-of-factly.

'I may not be able to defend the magazine singlehandedly, Fay. But I certainly can light up the biggest explosion the citadels of Delhi have ever seen!'

'Let us first find, Robert, Shah,' said Mastaan as the two men stepped out of mohalla Ballimaran.

'Yes, dada... if he is still safe that is. Things looked really bad at the Kashmiri Gate when I left,' replied Shahbaaz.

'Do not say that, Shah. We have to ensure his safety. I cannot return to Fay with more bad news at such a time. She loves him like a father.'

As they looked for the shortest way towards the powder-magazine, Mastaan held back Shahbaaz with an arm on his friend's shoulder.

'I am doing this for my love, for my Fay, Shahbaaz. Not sure why you are going through with it, brother...'

Shahbaaz grinned, but it showed only in his eyes behind his cloaked face.

'I don't call you *dada*, or big brother, just like that, Bandookbaaz. I am standing here today because of you. I owe you my life not once but many times over. And I know if it was me in your place and you in mine, you would have stood by me shoulder to shoulder. In any case, dada, in this madness of blood and gore, who knows what is right and what is wrong? If protecting a loved one is wrong, then we are all wrong in some manner or another.'

The last few words from Shahbaaz worked like balm on Mastaan's torn conscience. The simplicity with which his friend and protégé had outlined the situation was just what the long-haired warrior needed at this time.

Protecting a loved one can never be a wrong choice.

'They are all escaping to the Flagstaff Tower on the Delhi Ridge.'

On their way towards the powder-magazine building bordering the erstwhile palace of the Mughal prince Dara Shukoh, Shahbaaz had met one of his co-cavalrymen from the D'Cruze Regiment. The man was among the few remaining Indian soldiers who had still not been consumed by fanatical hate for the British.

The rider informed Shahbaaz that the situation at the Kashmiri Gate was worsening. Several officers including Robert D'Cruze and young company commander Edward

Vibart were attempting to escape the battle-scene which had begun to look more like a slaughterhouse. The rest of surviving English officers, soldiers, civilians and families had made their way to the Flagstaff Tower - a small, lone military outpost further up from Metcalfe House on the forested ridge.

'They are taking refuge there, Mastaan dada. Must be a couple of dozen English officers, soldiers and their women and children. I believe boys from the Anglo-Indian schools are standing guard at the battlements of the Tower. I am sure Leftinant Robert saahab will also make his way to it. He is nothing if not a survivor!'

'Yes, but they will not last long, Shah,' replied Mastaan. An astute solider and military commander, the Bandookbaaz knew that the Flagstaff Tower was on a high mound and in direct line of gun and cannon-fire. One raid by the freedom army would have led to an inescapable, horrible massacre.

'Yes, dada... but that at least gives us some time. Chhagan and hundreds of his men are marching towards the magazine building. That has to be our first priority.'

'You are right, Shah. It is now or never. Just remember what we discussed about the powder-magazine.'

Shahbaaz nodded.

'Yes, dada... we capture and defend the arsenal till Company reinforcements arrive...

...or we put the whole building on fire.'

SOS

Delhi, 1215 hours, 11th May 1857

'We must run for our lives!' exclaimed Pilkington, as the deafening noise of musket shots and crude bombs tore through the East India Company's telegraph office.

Despite offering this sensible suggestion to his teammates, Pilkington did not leave his own Morse-code station.

Assistant Operator Brendish was not in complete disagreement with his colleague. By now it was public knowledge that Europeans were being killed by the hundreds. It would be any minute now that a thousand-strong multitude of Indian sepoys would storm the telegraph building and burn it down with its occupants inside. Their superior, Charles Todd, had left the office in the morning and had still not returned. It was now up to these two men.

'Let us hang in here till we can, Pilkington,' replied Brendish. 'We will escape promptly in time if we hear of any mob approaching us. But before we leave, we must send out the latest information about this goddamned mutiny to the Commander-in-Chief General Anson. Perhaps also to the cantonments in both the Punjab as well as the Northwest Frontier.'

Pilkington agreed. The duo stayed on in the telegraph office till well past the afternoon. They later made their way to the Flagstaff Tower only in the nick of time.

But just as they had planned, two Morse code messages were hurriedly tapped out to the Ambala cantonment before they left the office. This SOS message describing the terrifying state of Delhi and the heavy British casualties reached General George Anson in no time, even as he was enjoying the cool heights of the British summer capital in Shimla. Much as Lord Canning had always feared, Anson's response was going to be frustratingly slow and indecisive.

The SOS message was, however, further forwarded to other chhaavanis like Lahore.

And Peshawar.

Peshawar, 1245 hours, 11th May 1857

He sat on a canvas field-chair behind the large desk placed in the middle of his battle-tent. A home meant nothing to him. He lived on horseback and slept in the saddle. A tent was a rare luxury that he permitted himself when he was not chasing a bandit horde across the barren hills of Northwest India and the borders of wild Afghanistan.

The forces of nature seemed to have no effect on him – heat, rain, sandstorms, snow... his bestial constitution was immune to every onslaught. Even deep wounds from enemy-axes and musket-shots had little more effect than that of a fleabite on this phenomenon of a man.

He wore nothing more than his uniform pants held up by leather suspenders stretched over his splendidly gigantic, sweating, muscular torso. A hand-gun was stuck into his waist belt and a cold beer lay in front of him in a glass tumbler.

There were other glass containers also on his desk, giving company to the innocent beer.

Immersed in large transparent jars filled with preservative formaldehyde, were the severed heads of North West Frontier's conquered warlords.

The most recent addition to this collection being that of Abu-Zar Pasha, the Lion of Peshawar.

The Azzami's head floated in an ominous glass barrel placed like a decorative piece on the tent-owner's table. This chilling, savage practice of this Brigadier General of the East India Company was as fearfully notorious as he himself was.

As he read the telegraph message, his jaw tightened involuntarily.

His eyes now glowered like embers as he read the news about the killing of British officers, women and children.

In the very next instant, he kicked his massive desk, toppling it over with a loud creak and a heavy thud... sending his decapitated trophies rolling on the sand now wet with the stench of stale formaldehyde.

'YAAAAARRRRGGGHHH...!' he screamed; his hands stretched out like claws.

His bloodcurdling cry was audible across the entire sandy cantonment of the East India Company. In a matter of seconds, it had ignited the heart of every soldier of his army. Unexplained as it was, John Nicholson had a magical, trance-like impact on his men – *Nikhaal Sena*, or Nikhaal's Army as it was called.

Among half a dozen other formidable British officers that were now preparing to march on Delhi and avenge the mutiny eye for an eye, the most dreaded one was seething in Peshawar.

Fate was paving the way for 1857's most frightful duel.

None other than *Nikhaal-bhagwaan,* the God Nikhaal, himself had sworn deadly revenge.

The Black Shadow

Delhi, 1245 hours, 11th May 1857

The magazine building was packed to capacity.

Even the largest army of the world could have provisioned itself from this inexhaustible supply of destruction paraphernalia. Field guns, rifles, muskets, cannon-balls, gun-grape, powder, shells... the place was a game-changer in every sense. Chhagan Dubey and the other unofficially accepted leaders of the ghadar were well aware that they had this war-treasure within their grasp. Control of the magazine meant an unlimited supply of counter-strike explosives to break the back of even the most crippling siege that was surely coming.

Under normal circumstances it appeared to be heavily guarded. But not today, when numerical strength had assumed an all new meaning. One hundred fully-armed guards would have been a strong deterrent on any other occasion. But when wave after wave of fighters, comprising three hundred trained infantry and cavalry each, advanced towards it with the determined goal to seize control of the arsenal, the equation became hellishly adverse for the British.

And when the attacking forces were being led by a seasoned and now-belligerent commander like the Subedaar-Major of the D'Cruze Regiment, swift fall of the magazine was imminent.

With that the fate of the East India Company, and of British rule in Hindustan, would have been sealed forever.

But for one man.

A man in love. A man who had sworn to protect his beloved even from the Gods.

He who altered everything on that fateful day.

Did one man really change the course of history's greatest war for freedom?

Lieutenant Willoughby, an officer of the Bengal Ordnance Department of the East India Company, was overwhelmed at the sight of the native sepoy legions that advanced towards his stronghold at the magazine. Along with Deputy Assistant Commissary Buckley, Conductor Scully and six other British officers, he was responsible for the defense of the magazine.

Ever since the Tilangas had ridden into the walled city, Willoughby had expected an attack on the prized treasure under his guard. But that it would come so soon and with such strength and vehemence was something he had not envisaged. He quickly ordered the gates of the magazine to be barricaded and placed two 6-pounder cannons double-charged with iron-grape aimed towards the mutineers. Another powerful

24-pounder howitzer, manned by John Buckley, was moved into position.

The attack was vicious. Rebel sepoys assaulted the magazine with dazzling battle prowess and a visible killer-instinct. They had decided to take over the magazine no matter what the cost. To add to the trouble of the British officers in command was the refusal of their native troops to fight against the rebels. In no time, most of their own native soldiers had abandoned the magazine and had joined forces with the attackers.

It was now two thousand fighters of the rebel army - against nine British officers, two cannons, one howitzer...

...and a masked Gunman.

The 6-pounder grape-cannon tore into the ranks of the advancing rebel army that charged forward fearlessly, deeply impressing the European defenders with their selfless valor. Conductor Scully was operating the smoking hot guns, assisted by the officer in command, Lieutenant Willoughby. Together they had succeeded in keeping the mutineers at bay for over an hour since the attack had begun. But slowly, the advance was becoming stronger and the grip of the attackers tighter.

Several native troops still stood inside the magazine compound and as Willoughby bent down to lift another parcel of explosives, a native sepoy charged at him with a drawn dagger. Before Willoughby realized what had happened and before the dagger could pierce his spine, the attacker fell dead, shot in the neck by a high-precision musket shot.

As Willoughby turned to look at the shooter who had just saved his life, he did not know what to make of him. His savior was not dressed in Company uniform. Nor was he in the typical white kurta, pajama and turban of the rebel army.

The man stood against one of the large open windows of the magazine overlooking the Jumna, his long tresses flowing with the strong river-breeze. His armor was black, so was the rest of his clothing. His face was painted in the deep grey of gunpowder burn. He was armed from head to toe with a long sword, two short battle-axes and two hand-pistols fastened across his belt and armor. Two more rifles were in the tight grip of his hands, one of the barrels smoking with the last shot fired.

'I am on your side... *today*.'

This was all that the young voice from behind the black veil said to the panting British officers, before swinging around and shooting dead two more rebels trying to place scaling ladders on the window behind him.

The fierce battle continued unabated.

Two hours had passed since the attack on the powder-magazine had begun. Both sides were stunned to see the grit and bravery of the other. The Indian soldiers were charging relentlessly towards the magazine even in the face of cannon and howitzer fire. The British officers were holding fort despite being horribly outnumbered.

It was a painful demonstration of the indomitability of the human spirit. But sadly, and as always in war, with no eventual winners.

Apart from the determined and shining gallantry of the nine British officers, what enabled the magazine defenders to hold it for four long hours even against a sea of enemy soldiers was the dazzling presence of Mastaan – who had kept wave after wave of the freedom army at bay with his unparalleled marksmanship. Every shot fired by Mastaan meant a headshot in the enemy ranks.

'Load faster!' instructed Mastaan to the British soldier who was deployed only to pass on loaded rifles to the Bandookbaaz. By now all sides of the magazine-building were being scaled by the freedom fighters using bamboo ladders. Shahbaaz and Conductor Scully were walking from window to window, cutting down any attacker who tried to enter the building. Buckley was manning the howitzer, pounding the mutineers with heavy shells.

But despite Mastaan's shower of fatal shots and Shahbaaz and other British officers' intense struggle, they could sense that the battle was more or less lost. The numbers of the rebel army were so daunting that these handful of men could not have held them back for much longer.

Minutes later, the heavily barricaded gate of the magazine creaked with a yawning rusty noise. Mastaan looked over from the window above the gate, only to find twenty or thirty rebel soldiers powering the gate open with their sheer collective muscle power. Breaking of the gate would have meant immediate defeat for the magazine defenders.

Without wasting a moment, Mastaan took a few steps back, drew his sword, ran up to the window and leapt off – diving straight into the thick of the enemy collective at the gate a floor below. In a matter of seconds, the Bandookbaaz had scrambled up to his feet and had shot one rebel soldier in the chest with his hand-gun and slashed the ribs of another with his sword. Soon it was Mastaan alone with his back against the iron gate and a large pack of angry Hindustani soldiers surrounding him from three sides.

These were easy odds for him.

Pardon me, my brothers, my countrymen... I do this for love.

With tears of anguish in his eyes, Mastaan launched a lethal counterstrike on the soldiers around him. He drew out one of his short battle-axes, twirled it expertly in his hand before tearing open the chest of the soldier closest to him with it. The unfortunate soldier fell with a shriek, blood sprinkling out of his body. Mastaan now pranced around in the limited space he had, confusing his opponents with his unpredictable maneuvering. Then, with one swift action of his right hand, he ripped through the throat of another attacker with his sword. In the very next instant, he was back to his prancing. A rebel took aim with his musket at the black-clad fighter, only to be hit squarely on his forehead by Mastaan's axe, slicing his head half-way into his brain.

With three summary killings in a matter of seconds, the soldiers began to pull back from the magazine gate, slowly but surely.

It was now that Balram turned to Chhagan. They were mounted on their horses, observing the proceedings from a distance.

'We have to stop this mysterious man, Chhagan dada. It is because of him that the magazine is still in British hands. He must have shot at least a hundred of our fighters. Who could he be, dada? A mercenary hired by the Company Bahadur...?'

'May be, Balli...' responded a thoughtful Dubey, perched on his horse like a General.

'Although it seems like I have seen this fighter before,' he said.

'His battle moves look oddly familiar.'

'You just changed the destiny of Hindustan, my friend...'

Delhi, 1500 hours, 11th May 1857

The deafening thunder of the howitzer and the cannons continued amidst a shower of blood and bullets.

As Mastaan was preparing to climb one of the ladders back up to the magazine's higher floor, a horseman charged at him at terrifying speed, swinging his sword menacingly. The Bandookbaaz's heart skipped a beat as he saw the rider's face.

Chhagnu... my brother.

The ex-Subedaar Major of the D'Cruze Regiment had decided to challenge the shadowy black fighter himself.

Mastaan could have shot down the approaching aggressor with great ease. His second pistol was still in his belt, loaded and ready to be fired. But it was Chhagan!

The Bandookbaaz had to get out of this one duel without anyone getting hurt.

As Chhagan galloped past, he slashed his sword at Mastaan with savage precision. In an instant it was clear that he meant business and was here to eliminate this unexpected speed-breaker in the way of their magazine capture. The long-haired fighter threw himself back with lightning speed to avoid Chhagnu's gleaming blade, the former's spine bent almost like a horseshoe.

But the assault was far from over. Chhagan Dubey slowed down his gallop and turned his horse around. He could not believe his eyes when he saw the black-warrior standing erect, unharmed. Such precise attacks from him seldom missed their target. That was not normal, Chhagan thought.

How is he still standing, totally unhurt? No one can escape such a close attack...

Except one man...

He shed the gnawing doubt. It could not be.

Chhagan spurred his mount again. He was charging back for a second and decisive attack.

As the Subedaar-Major's stallion pounded towards Mastaan, the Bandookbaaz had only one option left.

He stood in direct line of the mount's charge and drew his sword. Chhagan was happy to see this. He always preferred an equal fight.

But he was wrong.

This was not an equal fight. Much as Chhagan Dubey was a formidable fighter, standing on the other side was Hindustan's most unconquerable warrior – Mastaan!

In one calculated move, Mastaan drew his sword, held it above his head with both hands and took aim.

In the very next second, the sword had travelled through air like a bullet, piercing clean and length-long into the muscular thigh of Chhagan's massive horse.

The horse neighed in agony, bolted mid-gallop, throwing its rider headlong into the dusty road ahead.

Relieved that Chhagan was mostly uninjured, the Bandookbaaz swiftly climbed up the ladder, screaming to Lieutenant Willoughby... and making sure that his friend Chhagan also heard him loudly and clearly.

'NOOOOOWWW!! Lieutenant... light the gunpowder NOOOOWWWW!'

For a moment, stunned as he was from the harsh fall, the Subedaar-Major could not grasp what the black fighter was shouting.

But it did not take the soldierly instinct within Chhagan Dubey long to understand what was happening. As the gallant Lieutenant Willoughby took off his hat and swung it as a signal to his brave officers Buckley and Scully, Chhagan screamed at the top of his voice, cautioning his soldiers as loudly as he could.

'BHAAAAGOOOO...!'

'RUN!'

'RUUUU...NNN!'

He clambered up to his feet and darted away from the magazine, as fast as his legs could carry him. In this commotion, Balram and several other sepoys also caught on to the Subedaar-Major's warning and scrambled away from the battle site.

But not all the valiant Indian rebels were as fortunate as Chhagan and Balram.

In a matter of the next few seconds, the entire powder-magazine blew up in an explosion so loud that it shattered the glass chandeliers of the Laal Qila miles away, and its earsplitting sound could be heard as far as forty miles, even at the Meerut chhaavani. Along with the magazine, blown to smithereens were most of the selfless British officers in the building and over one thousand martyrs of the freedom army.

The end of this battle was as much a testimony to the bravery of the men on both sides as was its beginning. Mastaan, Shahbaaz and the nine British officers had set light to a gunpowder train willingly, knowing well that they would perish in the resulting detonation. The freedom fighters had anyway put their lives on the line, braving a storm of iron and fire all through the day.

Even though Chhagan had covered quite some distance before the magazine exploded, the earth-shattering eruption threw him off his feet and sent him flying several meters into the ignited air and ash ahead.

In one stroke, the freedom army had lost its greatest asset. In one stroke, the scale had tipped completely in the East India Company's favor. By fighting for just three hours against his own motherland, Mastaan had ensured a few more days or weeks or maybe even years of safety for Fay.

But in doing so, the patriot of Delhi had fallen.

Knowingly or unknowingly, Mastaan had altered the course of destiny. A nation that could have liberated itself from foreign yoke in 1857, had been shoved back into slavery because one man chose love above everything else.

As Chhagan watched explosion after explosion erupt in what remained of the burning magazine building, he was convinced who the black fighter was. They had spent too many years together on the battlefield for him to not know the signature combat moves of the magnificent Mastaan.

Seething with rage and reeling in pain from his scalded skin, clenching his teeth in an ashen mouth and with a tearing heart, Chhagan Dubey could only say a few exasperated words.

'*Oh, Mastaan baba... what have you done?*

You just changed the destiny of Hindustan, my friend...'

11th of May 1857

One of the bloodiest days in the tumultuous history of the mystical and ancient city of Delhi. Ravaged repeatedly by foreign marauders like Timur the Lame and Nadir Shah, the metropolis believed to have been first established as Indraprastha by none other than the mighty Pandavas, was perhaps the city destroyed and rebuilt the greatest number of times in world history.

However, on this day Delhi was burnt and bathed in blood by its own children, by its own residents. While the fateful date of the 11th of May witnessed the Great Uprising and the genesis of India's first war for independence, it also led to a genocide that made every street, every square and every mohalla of Delhi tremble with shrieks and pleas of dying men, women and children.

What the perpetrators of these heinous deeds, criminals, hiding themselves behind crowds of true patriots, forgot was a very brutal reality...

...that a ghastly British retribution was coming.

Within a few days of the Great Mutiny, a mammoth army called the Delhi Field Force had begun to lumber towards the Mughal Capital. From the British Parliament in London to every single English newspaper – all corners of Great Britain were now demanding an eye for an eye, and death for death.

Inching closer to Delhi under the command of three savagely bloodthirsty officers of the East India Company was a force comprising Sikhs, Gurkhas, princely armies, cannons, howitzers and thousands of infantry and artillery.

Delhi was going to be turned into a graveyard. Yet again.

Betrayed as it appeared to be by one of her ablest sons, the city was going to be razed to blood and dust by the God Nikhaal-bhagwaan, the Executioner William Hodson and the Reaper, the one-eyed Metcalfe.

What were the old Badshah Zafar's three ghoulish wishes?

Who was the terrifying half-faced dervish?

How was the haunted treasure of Tipu Sultan tied to this tale?

What happened to Fay and her Bandookbaaz?

Did Mastaan really change the course of the Great Mutiny singlehanded?

Did he ever fight for his motherland?

To be concluded...

1857

The Sword of Mastaan

by

VINEET BAJPAI

ABOUT THE AUTHOR

Vineet Bajpai is one of India's most popular and commercially successful authors. Counted among the 75 greatest Indian writers of all time, his books have touched the hearts & lives of millions of readers worldwide.

An HT-Nielsen chart-topping author, Vineet has written six books before *Mastaan*. His business and inspirational books *Build From Scratch* (2004), *The Street to the Highway* (2011) and *The 30 Something CEO* (2016) have been highly acclaimed.

Vineet's fiction novels, the best-selling *Harappa Trilogy*, sold over 1.5 lac copies within 18 months of release and are counted amongst the biggest successes in the history of Indian fiction.

Screen-rights of the *Harappa Trilogy* have been acquired by one of the largest film production houses in India. A regular speaker at the Jaipur Literature Festival and other international literary events, Vineet's books have been translated into several languages.

Mastaan - The Fallen Patriot of Delhi is Vineet's seventh book.

www.vineetbajpai.com
facebook.com/vineet.bajpai
twitter/vineet_bajpai
instagram/vineet.bajpai
Write to Vineet at - vb@vineetbajpai.com